A
Fairy's
Light

STEPHEN PHILLIPS

This story is a work of fiction. Any similarities to names, people, places are purely coincidental.

DEDICATION

To all my family and friends. To those who understand that the world is much more than what we think we can see.

Table of Contents

Chapter One

Frost hung in the air, its opalescence leaving a glowing trail as a small flicker of light quickly motioned through the tall trees. The light circled each, and as it did, vines that clung to them moved and unwound with whisper words only the forest would understand.

"You naughty vines, you hurt the trees. You warty things, leave them be!"

Her words rang through the air like a whispering bee as her light flickered, looping her way around all of the tall trees. Leaves moved, vines untangled, and when all was done the small creature hung like dust in the breeze floating before the forest. Roween was tired. She'd been working since the light of the sun shone over the horizon.

"Well, that's done, let me see. Not much fun, but where to be?"

She looked at her work, seeing the vines untangle from most of the trees. She knew that not all vines were jealous of the trees; many ran along the ground. They knew they would grow and didn't mind the forest floor. With a bow, she waved and thanked them for not tormenting her friends.

A breeze blew past, making Roween look to the sky as the trees above her dipped and swayed, but not from the winds; instead from sylphs that danced along their crowns. She gave a smile as the breeze slowed and the air again became still. They waved to Roween as they perched happily on the leaves. Roween had been busy weaving between the trees, and since there was no moon for the night, she knew her light could be seen. The sylphs reminded her of that, and she chided them as they gave their warning. Roween only smiled. She had faced many dangers before. She knew how to stay hidden when needed. After all, she had been alive since before humans walked the forest.

Suddenly, Roween looked around. She remembered where she was supposed to be.

"Oh, no, no, no, I had forgot to be somewhere that I am not."

With great speed, she flew quickly away. She darted through the trees, her direction true and straight; well, as straight as could be in a forest full of trees. Roween had forgotten about meeting her friend at her tree; she had asked the girl to help hide her door.

"The time was fast and gone too soon. But I never last, and fit to boon," Roween said as she rushed to her goal, hoping to meet her friend with time to spare. But as she approached, she saw no one standing by her tree she called home. *Is my friend late?* she thought.

Slowing, she turned around the large oak only to pause, seeing her friend on the ground by the base of her tree, covered in leaves.

"Amanda, Mandy, as sweet as can be. Amanda, so fancy, so good to see."

She flew beside her. The girl had been friends with Roween since arriving in the forest with her family. Roween had guided her back to safety when she became lost and the two had been friends ever since. Roween sometimes liked to play tricks on her, but nothing harmful; she knew Amanda always liked to have fun.

Roween floated quietly toward Amanda and was about to yell

her name to wake her, but the smile of playfulness ran from Roween's face upon seeing the blood dripping down her friend's forehead.

"Mandy, Mandy, wake up, my dear! Mandy, Mandy, please, can you hear?" Roween yelled loud enough for the animals far away to hear, making some scurry away.

She touched her tree and he told her what had happened. How the girl had taken the door and was trying to find a place to hide it for her, but Amanda tripped and hit her head on the rock near his roots, and how he asked the sylphs to keep her warm by using his old, dry leaves. He told her that the door was lost on the forest floor. He reminded her that there were those who had been searching for such treasures, but Roween did not care about her door. Her friend Amanda was the only concern she had right now.

"Amanda, my dear, please wake up. Amanda, don't fear. Oh, my friend named Supp."

Roween tried to heal her, but in winter the forest wasn't alive as she needed it to be. The leaves were dry and decaying; she needed life in them to heal her friend. Maybe she could carry her . . . Roween feared injuring her, but she would if she had to. She was a fairy, stronger than any human could ever be.

Her problem had not gone unnoticed, and she heard the sylphs say something within the breeze. *"A man is here, and he may help; his air is clear, and no whelp. We'll bring him near, for him to help."*

"Then hurry, please, she needs to mend. Lead him, please, help my friend!" Roween replied.

There was a sudden breeze and the leaves swirled all around, hiding them from the rest of the forest. And then, in an instant, there was a line of leaves that headed out into the woods.

* * *

Ron was out ghost hunting; it'd been a hobby of his for ages. Tonight, after thirty years, he had hoped for a change of luck. He reminisced about the stories he'd heard when he was younger. The stories about these woods being haunted and cursed.

The night was cold. The leaves barely made a sound in the breeze until a sudden wind howled all around him, making him bundle up his collar. It was fast, and the air felt colder than usual, so he begrudgingly packed up his gear to head back to his cabin. As the wind blew, several of the sylphs smiled, and the wind seemed to push him along. He stopped when suddenly his face was filled with leaves.

Ron paused. The woods were still dark, and his equipment was becoming heavy. The cold air made his chest feel tight, and he began to wonder if he was going to become a new spirit to these so-called haunted maples.

He opened his canteen; thankful its contents weren't too cold yet. He figured the warm coffee it held would last him until he returned home. Suddenly, his eyes caught a flash of light, then another, like the flicker of—a *firefly*? he thought. The temperature was somewhere below freezing, so it couldn't have been. Softening his stare, he hoped to let his peripheral vision take over as he reached into his bag to grab his camera. When its cold metal touched his fingers, he quickly pulled it from the bag, turned it on, and looked through the viewfinder. He kept his other eye open, looking through the trees, and when he saw it again, he took a picture.

To his dismay, he had accidentally turned on the flash, and a bright-blue haze now filled his vision. His eyes were already accustomed to the dark for some time, and he was now blind as a bat. But as his vision returned, he saw something that he couldn't believe. Whatever he saw was now flying in loops. When it stopped and drifted gently between the trees, he stepped forward, trying to find good footing, but he was still unable to see clearly and then he heard a snap, making him look down. That in itself shouldn't have been anything to worry about. And as Ron smiled, seeing his breath hanging in the cold air, he again looked forward. That's when things became a little "unusual."

He stared at the small light, thinking, *Did I just scare a ghost?* But his smile quickly faded as the light raced toward him. It was fast, flying like a bird, but more agile. And after making a ninety-degree turn around a tree, it was now headed directly for him. He again raised his camera, hoping to get a picture, and pressed the shutter, this time remembering to close his eyes. The flash went off, and the small light stopped only feet away. It moved like a bug floating gently in the air.

"What is that?" he asked out loud.

He wasn't expecting an answer; at least nothing verbally. But then he heard something say, in a gentle, willowy, musical voice, *"Stop, with that flashy thing. Its light makes my eyes sting."*

He could only imagine the look on his face when it flew before him. Ron didn't breathe when he saw her, and yes, it was a person—a small, glowing person. She had translucent wings, and her silvery-white hair had a touch of green. Ron blinked his eyes several times as she floated there, still rubbing her own. He was about to say something, but stopped when she looked at him with those warm blue eyes.

"I'm in need of help, for my friend, you see. Please come and help. Please follow me," this tiny creature said in an urgent, musical way.

He followed her through the trees, not knowing why; but after a moment, he started thinking this was some kind of hallucination. Maybe it was a lack of sleep. Maybe he had finally lost his mind.

He was still out of breath from before, but his wits were returning, and he questioned why he was following this small, glowing person. He shook his head as he watched her stop and fly slowly in circles around a nearby tree before flying back to where he was.

"Hurry, hurry, there is no time. Hurry, hurry, please help a friend of mine!" Her voice became urgent, but strong.

And as she grabbed the strap of the pack he was carrying, he found out just how strong she was as she pulled him forward with such force that his feet left the ground. This little person was much stronger than someone twice his size.

"Hurry, hurry, worry, worry!"

She's still rhyming, was all he thought.

It was amusing until he saw what looked like a small girl lying on the ground by a tree. His wits came back in an instant and he rushed over, seeing the blood on her head. Quickly he looked her over then grabbed a lens cloth, placing it gently over her wound. He yelled for her to wake up. She moved, but only a little, so he shook her very gently and yelled again.

"Worry, worry, hurry, hurry!" his small, glowing friend said as she swooped down, touching the girl's nose as if trying to wake her.

"Please wake up, friend named Supp!" she said loudly.

He yelled for her to wake up again; this time, she opened her eyes. But as she focused on him, she started to scream and scurried away. She was frightened. He couldn't blame her; a stranger, in the woods, late at night . . . we've all heard the stories.

Amanda curled up next to the tree and grabbed a nearby stick, holding it before her. She tried to speak, but her words stumbled;

she was frightened, and injured, so Ron stayed where he was.

His concern grew when he saw the blood again start to run down her forehead. He could see the tears in her eyes. He wanted to help; she could have easily been his daughter. She couldn't have been more than ten. But every time he moved, she shrank back into the tree.

He watched as the little glowing woman flew before her. The girl's eyes remained focused on him as he heard, *"Friend named Supp, you're on the ground. This is help I have found. I know you're scared, but please know true. This man is fair, and friend to you."*

Her words sounded comforting, even to him, so he inched closer and introduced himself. "My name is Ron; Ron Wilt."

He tried to sound comforting, but she still held him at bay. Then he saw something even more strange, as their small friend waved her hands and glittering powder flew from them. He watched as the young girl's eyes softly closed while she still remained focused on him.

The winged creature flew before him. *"You are fair and good. That I see. Please take Supp home for me. I made her sleep, but she is hurt. Please take her from the cold, wet dirt."*

He blinked his eyes and moved beside the girl, again placing his cloth over her wound. He was going to see if she would wake up, but the small creature flew before him.

"No, no, no, do not wake. Take her home, haste you make!" she said. He was still in wonder at her constant rhyming.

He looked the girl over again, making sure she wasn't injured worse than before, and then carefully wrapped her in the blanket from his pack before picking her up. He stood, holding her in his arms, and looked around, confused. "I don't know where she lives."

"Follow me, come, come, come. Hurry, hurry, before the sun!" she urged, pointing at the now glowing horizon. *"I will lead your way; please watch that stone. I'll lead your way to take her home."*

He followed the glow from his winged guide to a cabin with what looked like some very worried parents rushing around outside. Ron yelled to get their attention and they quickly ran over, grabbing their daughter from him. Her father pushed him back. "What'd you do to her?" He was obviously angry.

"Easy . . . I found her like this. I stopped the bleeding as best I could," he said, trying to keep things calm.

Her mother focused on Amanda as her father confronted him. Thankfully, that's when the police arrived. Ron spent the next few hours explaining that he had been taking pictures in the woods looking for ghosts, even hearing an officer say, "Oh, you're one of *those* freaks."

The girl finally woke and told them what had happened. She confirmed his story, although the police didn't seem to want to believe her, either. Ron stayed silent; in his defense, babbling about some small, glowing, winged creature wouldn't have helped his case.

The ride in the police car wasn't bad; he'd never been in one before. He knew things would be fine—any evidence they had was circumstantial at best. But he did call his lawyer, just to be safe. It took a few hours, and after repeated questioning, and the girl telling them that a friend saved her, they finally let him go. Ron wouldn't have blamed them if they had held him; there were always stories on the news where things didn't turn out well. Besides, how would he explain that a small, flying, glowing woman had led him to her?

It was night when he arrived back at his cabin and wearily, he dropped his pack on the ground before closing the door. In the kitchen, he splashed some water on his face; the cold felt refreshing, but also filled his eyes with water. Grabbing a towel to dry off, he leaned his head back, but when he opened them . . . that's when everything stopped and his breath froze. His eyes were now staring at a small, glowing, winged woman before him. In a panic, he fell backward, looking for any escape; but when turned back, he saw nothing. Meeting her in the forest was one thing, but in his cabin? That was scary.

Quickly, he rose from the floor and headed into the living room. He thought, *Am I going insane?* But he calmed himself and dropped onto the worn sofa. Shaking his head in frustration, he again closed his eyes. That's when he heard, *"Friend Ron, I know you're true. Supp is safe because of you."*

He opened them to find himself again staring at a small, glowing figure floating before him. He rubbed his eyes, hoping this was a dream.

"No dream, friend Ron, your sight is true. I'm here to convey the mantle of friend to you."

"Ooooookay," he said, not believing what he was hearing.

"Thank you for your act of kind. I know troubles now weight your mind. But please know this, nothing's amiss, nothing is wrong, friend Ron. Your troubles are gone. They all now forget, for fairy dust they have all met." It was mesmerizing, her ability to speak in rhyme.

"Uh, thanks," was all he could manage to say. After all, he was speaking to a . . . fairy?

"You are real? Am I actually seeing you?" he asked, hoping to hear a "no" answer.

"Yes, you can see. Yes, yes, you can see me, a fairy." She smiled and glowed brightly, spinning in a pirouette before him.

"All right, so if I can see you, what do I call you?" he asked, amazed at how quickly he accepted her existence.

She didn't respond, but instead looked around, almost as if scared, before heading to the window. Ron watched as she flitted to each side of it, making him follow her. And as he walked to where she was, thinking, *what am I doing?* she flew here and there, as though scared to be in one spot for too long. But she remained focused on something in the forest. She turned to him and said, "*I have no time; they will find.*"

"Who will find you?" he asked.

"*No, no, not me they find; my home, my home. Please, no time!*" she said and grabbed him by the shirt, pulling him out the door. She was just as strong as before and dragged him out into the dark woods. Ron was thankful he hadn't had a chance to remove his jacket. But when he asked where they were going, all she said was, "*Hurry, hurry, please no time. Hurry, hurry, or they'll find.*"

He followed her as fast as possible, pausing only to turn to see if he could still see the lights from his cabin. They were close enough that he could find his way back in the dark, and it was only a little farther before they stopped. He was out of breath, and she flitted before him looking around, worried. Just as he started to ask her what was wrong, they heard a loud *snap* in the forest before them.

Something, or someone, heavy stepped on a branch nearby and she flew close to him. "*Worry, worry, where to flee? Worry, worry, or they'll see!*"

She searched for someplace to hide, making Ron shrug his shoulders before opening his jacket, offering her the pocket inside. She hesitated, but smiled before saying, "*Near your heart; that is good. The fabric parts as it should.*" She then flew in and looked up at him. "*Please, oh please, find my door; it fell onto the forest floor. It's shiny and round with a hint of red. Please find it now, or they'll make me dread."*

He didn't know what she was talking about, but as he searched through the leaves, he found what looked like a small mirror on the ground so he picked it up and showed it to her. He could see her eyes open wide as she smiled ear to ear, nodding her head. *"You've found my door, now I can breathe! They hound me poor, for them to see. Hide it, hide it, please make haste. Hide it, hide it, someplace safe."*

Then Ron noticed movement in the darkness before them and placed the mirror in his pocket. He watched as before them appeared a man with a night-vision rig on his head. Ron quickly moved away from her tree and confronted him.

"What are you doing in my yard at this hour?" he demanded sternly.

Ron surprised the man who jumped back, falling painfully onto some branches as he landed. Ron couldn't help but laugh when the man replied, "It's none of your business."

Ron told him, "It is my business, since this is my land."

He asked what Ron was doing out in the woods. Ron simply answered, "Chasing you off my property."

The man spoke into his radio, and several of his friends came to his aid. Most also carried electronic equipment, and were surprised when Ron confronted them as they appeared.

"What are you doing out here in my yard?" he asked again, sounding angry.

"We're looking for something," one of them responded.

"I don't care, get off my land!" Ron yelled, making some of them jump. "I live up here and I don't want you messing around on my property."

"Hey, old man, we have every right to be here. Besides, we—"

One of his friends interrupted him, showing him something on the display. "No, we don't; there's nothing here. We're not getting any readings," he told him. The young man before him looked around. "We should probably look in that direction," he said, and started to walk away."

"Hey, that doesn't look like a radiation detector. You should be careful. There was a mine around here that was supposed to have closed because they found uranium. Don't want you guys glowing in the dark," Ron said with a laugh.

Several of them were frightened by his statement and rushed away. The one he met earlier soon followed, and he watched as they disappeared back into the forest. Then Ron felt movement by his chest and opened his jacket. When he did, out popped the fairy. She looked in the direction they'd gone, and turned back with a smile.

"Gone, they're gone. Thanks to your lie. Gone, they're gone, and goodbye." She jetted up before him, spinning as she did.

Ron removed the mirror from his pocket. She gently inspected it, and nodded an "all right." *"You saved me, friend Ron, for that is sure. My thanks and happiness so do soar. But a favor once more, I ask of you. I hope you're braver when all is through. My home is here in that tree. Please help hide my door for me. Somewhere safe, not found, for me to hide, not plainly seen on any side."*

"So, you want me to help hide your door so they won't find it?"

She confirmed this statement with a nod, and Ron looked around for a safe place to put her door. He moved some leaves from a branch that hung on her tree and noticed what looked like a small hollow where a branch had broken off long ago; the opening was just big enough for the mirror to fit. He asked if this was a good place. She nodded in excitement, and he slid the mirror into its new hiding place, away from prying eyes. She darted to it and entered the knot; he watched as her light disappeared, only to have her appear moments later, happily flitting about in the air before him.

"*Thank you, thank you, that is lovely. Now no one but only you or I can see.*" She flew up to him, planting a gentle kiss of thanks on his nose. He couldn't help but smile.

He watched as she flew around from tree to tree, whispering things he couldn't hear. She flew back and spun before his eyes. She seemed happy, and flew down to the ground to pick a small blue flower, which he hadn't noticed, before giving it to him. "*I told my friends, the other trees, about the things you did for me. They are tall and tower, and asked me to give you this beautiful flower.*"

He smiled even more in disbelief. He didn't know why; maybe it was the lack of sleep, or the realization that he was talking to an actual fairy. He smelled the flower and thanked her. She smiled back, her light brighter now.

"Wait, I don't know your name. What do I call you?" he asked, realizing once again that she'd never answered the times before.

She flew to the flower he held and landed on it. She curtsied. "*My name is Roween, now you be know-eeng,*" she said with a giggle. He couldn't help but laugh. It was a bad rhyme, but her delivery was flawless.

Her smile was calming and wonderful, like the forest sometimes is, and he felt the cool air sweeping in as darkness gave way to dawn. "*It's almost dawn; I have work to do. You should go; so do you.*"

She was right. He had pictures to take from the camera, and start that article on the haunted woods. He didn't know how to explain what he'd just experienced. Truthfully, he didn't think he wanted to, so he turned to leave.

"Wait, will I see you again?" he asked, and turned around.

Her voice was quiet, like a breeze of soft air. *"In three days' time will be my return; you will again hear my rhymes, do not concern,"* she said with a smile, and flew into her tree.

Ron headed back to his cabin and placed the small flower in a glass with some water and relaxed on the worn couch. The last day or so had been exhausting and with so much adventure, he fell asleep quickly.

When he awoke the next morning, stiff from lying awkwardly on that couch, he began to wonder. *Did I really see a fairy? Was I thrown in jail? Did any of this happen or was it just a dream?* He lifted himself up and stretched. He doubted the account of what had happened until he saw the blue flower in the glass beside the couch. He smiled and said, "Well, that clinches it for me; guess I really *did* see a fairy!"

Chapter Two

Ron thought it quite a story. In the past few days, he'd met a new friend, a fairy named Roween. He'd hoped she'd return, but as of lunchtime, she had yet to appear. *Maybe fairy time is different.*

He did miss her rhymes; her musical voice made it sound like she was singing. Ron sent the files he was working on to his editor and went for a walk, hoping maybe he'd see her near her tree. He was surprised to find himself excited by the hope of seeing her again, and it showed in his hurried steps. He was in such a rush that he forgot his coat, but thankfully, it was a warm day.

When he arrived, he took a good look around, making sure no one was near. He even knelt down to make it look like he was picking something up off the ground; then he picked up a stick and examined it, just in case. He finally saw the glimmer of her door and stared at it, hoping to see her fly from that silvery portal, but after several minutes, nothing.

As he waited, he began to scrounge the ground again as if looking for something, but after some time, found nothing. Disappointed, he brushed himself off and turned to head home, but as he did, his sleeve snagged on a thorn vine, tearing his shirt. He gave a sigh and looked at it, realizing he'd have to sew it together—but that wasn't all. As he closely inspected his newly ventilated shirt, he noticed the vine did more than tear the cloth, and watched as the red ooze of blood from his arm showed its tenacity. Thankfully, it wasn't bad, and he looked back at what had done the deed, still holding a sliver of cloth.

It wrapped around the tree, reaching out its tendrils. The vine hugged the tree so tight that it was crushing the bark. Ron threatened to come back and cut it away, laughing, realizing he was talking to a thorny vine strangling a tree. He wiped the blood from his arm and, seeing no more, headed home.

The cabin was quiet. He even whispered Roween's name to see if she was there, but there was no answer. "Guess she's not here," he said beneath his breath before heading to his bedroom. That's where he kept a small box with odds and ends, small things sometimes needed, like pins, pens, pencils, and of course needle and thread. He took the box from the shelf that ran along the entire wall and again spied the hole in it from when he'd put the shelf up years ago, promising for the dozenth time to fix it, someday, and proceeded to thread the needle and remove his shirt.

As he was sewing, something moved out of the corner of his eye. Hoping it was Roween, he said, "Is that you?"

There was no movement. He was thinking maybe he shouldn't hope so much to see her. Maybe she wouldn't be back as soon as he'd wanted, so again he focused on fixing the tear in his shirt. Then again, from the corner of his eye, he saw movement. But whatever it was, it was dark, not like he'd seen with Roween. The creature was on the shelf, and this time he watched as it moved along behind some items. Ron moved slow and steady, quickly placing the box on its side, blocking the entire shelf from front to back. Whatever it was stopped before shuffling here and there, knowing it was trapped.

Then, to his surprise, a mouse appeared on the book before the box. Ron shook his head. "It's only a mouse." He watched it scurry back and forth, as any mouse would when faced with an obstacle. It looked at him with small, dark eyes; dark like polished glass. "I'm not moving that box; you can find another way to your home."

The small creature paused as Ron returned to his task, pulling the thread tight on each pass. But then movement again caught his eye, making him look up, and he was surprised by what he saw. The mouse had a small rope of thread, the same he was using, and tossed it over the box. Ron was stunned.

"You're not a mouse!" Ron exclaimed. "And you're no fairy, either."

He heard a surly little voice exclaim, "You're right, I'm no fairy; they can fly over this blasted box."

Ron tilted his head in amazement and confusion, thinking, *Great, now what have I met?*

As Ron looked closer, the mouse turned to stare at him with its glass-like eyes. It took Ron a moment to realize they were actually glass, and in the light, he could see into the creature's mouth. He swore he could see . . . a face.

"All right, who, or what, are you?" Ron demanded.

Only a moment passed before he heard, "I'm no fairy, you big one."

Now things became even stranger. As he moved closer to get a better look, the tiny creature no longer moved like a mouse, but like a man. "All right, you caught me," the small man said, and removed the mouse head from atop his shoulders. He stood a whole five inches tall, with tussled brown hair, and was wearing a mouse head and suit. He stared at Ron with some annoyance before saying, "I'm trying to get back to my house, do you mind?" pointing to the box Ron had placed blocking his path.

Ron shrugged his shoulders, then removed it from the small

man's path. He was surprised as the creature said a graceful, "Thank you," and headed into the hole in the wall. Ron moved to see what he was doing and looked inside. Although the light from the window now allowed him to see more, he was suddenly surprised as two small figures appeared from the darkness.

"All right, you big one, you caught me. What do you want to do? I warn you, though, I can be a tough bugger. I'm not taking my leave of this here house very easy," the one holding the mouse head said while the other remained silent.

"I just asked who you were; I thought you were a friend," Ron said.

"A friend? You called me a fairy. I'm not one of those," the small man griped.

Ron watched as the other brought her hands to her mouth and in a delightfully feminine voice asked, "Did he say he was a friend of a fairy?"

"That he did, and he thought *I* was a fairy," the small man said with a laugh.

"That is why he noticed you, my love; he has eyes not just of this world," the other said.

"Does he now?"

The woman next to him looked up at Ron. He could see the green of her small eyes as she widened them and then squinted as she looked him over. "Aye, he has light in them. That's not good for us."

"Great. I see a fairy days ago, and now these . . . these . . ." Ron suddenly looked confused. "What do I call you?"

The small man moved forward, shaking his mouse head. "We are called many things—elves, which we're not; dwarves, not them either; nor pixies, nor borrowers; nor the like. We are what we are."

Ron rolled his eyes. He may have been confused and unaware as to what to call them, but he still didn't have an answer. "You didn't answer my question," he politely said.

"This is a smart one," the woman said.

"You're right, love. We are brownies, you big one," he replied.

"Well, that makes sense. But I thought brownies had fur on them," he noted, thinking back to stories he'd heard as a child.

"Of all the . . . you big idiot. Those are *forest* brownies. *They* have fur. Heck, they don't even bathe! We're house brownies. Nothing like 'em," was his surly reply.

"We are the spirits of this house. It's nice to meet you," the woman said politely, giving side-eyes to the man.

Her companion huffed and threw his mouse disguise down. "He's gonna be a problem for us now, you know that."

She shook her head. "I don't think he'll be a problem. He knows a fairy, doesn't he?"

The man put his hand to his chin and nodded. "You may be right. Guess we should introduce ourselves."

The woman walked forward and curtsied. "I am Josclyne. And this is my husband, Erant."

Then Erant bowed and waved his hand in a sort of salute. Ron returned the greeting, telling them his name.

"Ron or Ronald?" the woman asked.

"Ronald, but please call me Ron," he replied.

"It is nice to meet you, Ron. I hope you are comfortable here."

He was flattered by their now gracious attitude and formality toward him, but he did have some questions. When he said, "May I ask something?" Josclyne nodded.

"Are you the spirits who have been borrowing my TV remote when I can't find it?" He tried not to laugh at what he thought was a simple question, but Erant's reaction was something other than eloquent.

"Of course, you—mmmmph," was all he heard before the woman covered his mouth with her hand. "Yes, that box is loud when you're trying to sleep. Could you please not use it so much?"

Ron nodded and gave a laugh; he had solved the age-old question: "What happens to the remote when you can't find it?"

They spoke for a short time as Ron finished sewing his sleeve; it was a passable job, and he wouldn't have to buy a new shirt. Besides, he liked this shirt. As he tied the knot to finish up, he looked at them and said, "I can't believe I'm talking to brownies. Can't wait to tell Roween when she gets here."

"Who's Roween?" Josclyne asked.

"Oh, that's her name, the fairy I met a few days ago."

Her face turned red and she covered her mouth before she said with a smile, "The fairy gave you her name? When will she be here?"

He told them she was supposed to be here today, but that it was getting late.

"She will be here soon, I think. Fairies are not always good with time," she told him.

"Great, can't wait to hear nothing but rhyming when she gets here," Erant mumbled, his statement bringing a nudge from his wife.

"Don't be rude. Besides, if she told him her name, she has plans for him," she said with dream-filled eyes and a big smile.

The way she acted caused a chill in Ron, although for some odd reason, he wasn't sure it was a bad thing. They continued to talk for a few more minutes before his new friends insisted on returning to whatever they were doing. As he turned to leave, Ron heard, "Hey, big one. What're you making for dinner?"

His question brought another nudge from his wife. "You're being rude," she said.

Ron laughed, finding these two amusing, and hoped they'd stay, so he told them he was thinking of making pancakes for dinner because he hadn't done so in a while.

A flight in the breeze, and winds that blow.

Speak with the trees, so they will grow.

- Fairy saying.

Chapter Three

Roween held her hand to her tree. "*I thank you for your gift. I'll make it clean, and make it swift.*" With her other hand, she quickly pulled a string of bark from her tree. It came off in one piece, and she held it tight to her, closing her eyes. She spoke again, her words floating gently, making no sound—at least, none this world could hear. She then placed her hand on the freshly exposed wood. Opening her eyes slowly, she watched as moss grew where she touched, and in moments, it covered the spot where the bark once was.

She waved her hand as she drifted to the forest floor and three mushrooms quickly grew from the soft ground, lifting a small, flat rock from the earth. Gently she placed the bark on it, and skillfully formed it into a circle. The fibers were loose and frayed; she worked with intent, pulling on each strand carefully. Her hands worked fast, like the blur of a bug. Then, as if a flicker of sunlight, she applied some fairy magic. If not for the daylight, its brightness would have been a beacon for all to see. And as the glow of her magic faded, before her on that stone now sat a wooden ring with a cherry tone and fine grain.

She was pleased with her work, but far from done. Holding it before her, she said, "*This is for the true of heart, who never cower. Become the part of their true power,*" then tossed it into the air. However, unlike most things that fall when tossed, it floated before her, glowing softly, fairy magic drifting all around. "*Your way you find when you are lost, and hope that binds when this is tossed.*" She continued her enchantment, and as the last of the dust fell, it floated down to the table. She grabbed it, then placed it in a small satchel made of soft spider's silk. Then, with a leap, she headed for the sky above the leaves.

She looked toward the sun; it was lower on the horizon than she had thought. "*I'm late, I'm late, make haste, make haste.*" Quickly, she flew off toward Ron's cabin. As she did, she noticed the air was quiet, not as she remembered. Something was missing. An uneasy feeling slowed her pace. The air was cold. Not just the temperature; it lacked a warmth of life.

She stopped to look around, spying a few sylphs dancing on the leaves of nearby trees. She giggled remembering how her tree laughed when they tickled his leaves, and how sometimes they would sing. She floated slowly in the air, wondering why it felt strange, leaving herself exposed above the safety of the trees. This situation can be dangerous for a fairy; she knew that. But she didn't fear any bird or hawk or raven that may mistake her for a bug. She was a fairy. She was of the forest, and stronger than any of them. Even if she were to get into trouble, any sylphs nearby would come to her aid.

"*That is it, now I see. Bless my flit, that's the key!*"

She had finally figured out why the air seemed colder; there was less life in it. She counted them, the sylphs; that was the key. There had been so many, more than she remembered since she learned to fly, but now there were only a few dancing above the leaves. Quickly she flew to one nearby, but paused at what she saw.

The sylphs weren't dancing; they were searching. Some were flying, as all sylphs do; others were weeping as they sat on the leaves.

"*What is wrong, what is wrong? Your face so long, and no song,*" Roween asked.

A sylph looked up at her, transparent eyes filled with wistful tears. *"Our friends are gone, we don't know where,"* she said. *"We've searched the trees, the lakes, and air, but we cannot find them anywhere."*

Roween became concerned, then remembered the men from the night before. She also remembered others had gone missing after they had been in the woods. *Were they to blame for the disappearance of her friends? But this wasn't the first time others had gone missing.*

"I am friends with sylphs, and my concern, are there any elves or others gone? We must learn," Roween said.

She knew if those from before were involved, they needed to find them. This was a great concern for all of her kind.

Roween looked around and saw the smoke from Ron's cabin. It gave her an idea. *"I have a friend, and he may help. He's a trusted man, and no whelp."* She clutched the small bag and flew as fast as she could toward his cabin.

She stopped at the door, searching for the crack. That's how she'd entered after they met. She found it and went through.

In the kitchen, she saw him taking the kettle to the sink and filling it with water. She could smell the food, and it warmed her. There may have been trouble, but this made things feel better. She flitted softly, no sound at all. She turned the corner to see the stack of pancakes warming on the stove. *Is this for me?* she thought, and she glowed brighter. She held the silk bag tightly. *He is a good man, but first things first, I have a plan. Although things seem worst, I won't forget. Her hair of fire, he won't regret, they'll all admire.*

She then flew to a chair behind him, landing quietly on its back. He hadn't noticed her, but when he turned around: *"Pancakes are good, there's no meat. I like lots of honey, nice and sweet!"* she sang loudly.

Ron stumbled back against the counter, startled by her, but quickly recovered as she sat laughing on the chair before him.

Regaining his composure, he laughed, having expected her the entire day, and as soon as he turned his back, there she was. *This sprite is full of tricks,* he thought, also remembering he was dealing with someone only a few inches tall who could easily pull him along like someone twice his size.

The water began running out of the kettle and he reached over to turn off the faucet. He picked it up to pour some water out, then held it before her.

"Some tea with your pancakes?" he asked.

She nodded with that magical smile of hers.

He put the kettle on, then reached in the cabinet for some honey. He hadn't been using it himself for some time, preferring maple syrup. Looking at the bottle, he thought, *that should be enough for a fairy.*

Grabbing the stack of pancakes on the stove, he placed them on the table in the center of four settings, which brought a quizzical look from Roween, making Ron remember he hadn't yet told her. "We have guests—or maybe I'm the guest. Or since they were here when the house was built, maybe . . . I'll never figure this one out. We have more friends joining us for dinner." He was delighted that she seemed happy to hear that.

Moments later, Erant and Josclyne arrived wearing much more formal attire than they had earlier. As they jumped to the table, he introduced them. "This is Josclyne and Erant. They are the brownies of this house."

Josclyne curtsied and said, "Pleased to meet you, fairy friend."

Erant bowed, then gave his funny salute. "Yeah, great to see you." Ron laughed, seeing the mouse tail from his suit following behind the small man.

Roween stood properly and curtsied in kind. *"It's nice to greet, I am friend of Ron. I'm glad to meet, but fae or—fauna?"*

She covered her mouth to hide a giggle as she looked behind Erant. That made Josclyne look as well, and her response was the same. She covered her mouth before lovingly reaching behind him to unfasten his tail.

This made him say with a sneer, "I thought I'd forgotten something."

His wife assured him it was all fine; Roween acknowledged him, making light of the whole thing. She had a way about her that Ron thought could make a clock face laugh.

He offered pancakes to all. Erant and Josclyne would only accept one, and they were sharing. Roween, however, asked for five. He then began to wonder if she was humoring him asking for so many and offered them all honey, which they took. He opened the bottle and poured some for Erant and Josclyne, but when asking Roween she said, *"Mmmm . . . pancakes five, I'll take the hive."* She then motioned for him to pour as much of the honey as the plate would hold. There was only a little left, so he thought about getting some syrup from the refrigerator. But seeing the current company, he decided that there was more than enough for him.

Roween sat, her eyes glaring, lips smacking at the stack before her. Ron turned to check the kettle. When he turned back, he saw Josclyne and her husband using small forks to eat with, but when he looked at Roween, he saw something amazing. She reached her hands before her and in a single motion the pancakes, all of them, including the honey, pulled toward her open mouth. It was incredible, like they were pulled through an unseen straw, simply disappearing before her. He sat, eyes wide in amazement as she politely took the corner of the napkin and patted her mouth. He could swear the plate looked cleaner than when it was placed there.

She caught him staring, then sat tall. *"They were warm, and sweet, and very good. I ate them like any fairy would."*

He laughed. "That was a compliment if I ever heard one."

A few minutes passed. They all laughed when Erant told a joke, although Ron had to admit he didn't completely understand, but laughed. *Must have been magical creature humor.*

Halfway through their meal, Roween suddenly remembered something and reached into her bag. She then flew before Ron, holding a wooden ring. Ron looked at it as he took it from her. It looked very well made, such fine wood grain; it was almost as if it had been made by magic.

"This is for the true of heart, who never cower. Become the part, of their true power. Wear it on a chain of silver, in case of need, do not lose or quiver. Please my words need heed."

It took Ron a moment to realize what she was saying, but he grasped that this was meant to protect him in some way. It was flattering, and he graciously accepted it.

"Excuse me, is that made from your tree?" Josclyne asked.

Roween nodded.

Josclyne sat straight, knowing now for certain that Roween had plans for him. "But to have a ring of fairy wood, it must be dangerous," she whispered politely to her husband.

They'd had dealings with fairies before. There were always unseen plans; most were harmless and playful, but to have a ring of fairy wood, that meant it was serious. She now felt an uneasiness in Roween's gift, and was about to ask what else Roween wanted when the kettle whistled.

"I'm in time for tea; I like mine hot. Sweet and tasty, that's my lot."

Ron gave a quiet laugh before excusing himself. The moment Ron's back was turned, Roween flew before Erant and Josclyne. *"We need his help; that I'm sure. I ask your silence, please endure."*

Both nodded, then Josclyne asked, "Will it save him if he gets into trouble?"

Roween nodded, then motioned her hands in the form of the ring before sitting down.

"Good. You don't find many like him around."

Bringing the kettle back to the table, he set it down on a thick towel and placed a couple of tea bags in the pot to steep. He grabbed some cups acquired in his travels; they weren't fine china, but they were clean, and placed them on the table before sitting down to finish his meal. Roween told them how she made the ring, while waiting for everyone to finish. She even told Ron of how she noticed fewer sylphs than before; she seemed saddened when she mentioned them. He still couldn't put it past him that he now knew of at least three magical creatures in his woods, having never believed in magic before. Ghosts maybe, but never magic. That was, until that fateful night when he met her.

He finished his meal, as did the brownies, who sat politely waiting for him and their tea. He cleared the plates before pouring the well-steeped tea. Roween first, then he offered her the honey, which she quickly took and poured into her cup. As she placed it down, Ron started to pour the contents of the pot into the brownies' cup, but they stopped him, asking for much less, making Ron think, *I guess all magical creatures don't eat the same.*

Then, like a magician, Erant produced two small cups from

beneath his jacket, bringing jubilant applause from their fairy company. They dipped them in the larger cup and happily drank it as it was. When Roween's fanfare was done, Ron watched as she picked up the nearby spoon and flew in circles, stirring the honey into her tea. Ron couldn't help but smile as he poured his cup. It seemed so strange, but for some reason, normal—at least for present company.

They drank, and spoke; it was a surreal encounter. Erant told more jokes, they laughed, and a good time was had by all. Then Erant asked for one of the toothpicks that Ron had in the jar on the counter. When he reached for them, he snagged his sleeve on the back of his chair, popping the button through the loosened hole. As he handed the small jar to Erant and turned his attention to his now undone cuff, he pulled it back, making sure he hadn't pulled the button off, exposing the cut from earlier.

There was a loud thump as Roween dropped her cup to the table before flying to his arm. *"You are hurt; please make sure it's free of dirt."*

She had genuine concern in her eyes as she inspected his wound, although he felt more pain when she twisted his arm to have a better look. *"The wound is dry and not so runny; I'll fix it up with magic, and honey."*

She then took the bottle of honey and started to pour its contents over the cut. Ron tried to pull away, but couldn't; she held his arm fast in her grip. *"If you move, this will not work; please sit still, do not jerk."*

He couldn't move, even if he wanted to. She held his arm tight, and it was now also covered in honey. She dropped the bottle and waved her hand across the wound. There was a glow, and again what looked like dust, sparkling before it. He watched as her form lit brightly, then faded again, before releasing him with a smile. *"Your wound is sealed; now all is healed."*

Ron looked at where the cut used to be; there was nothing, with the exception of all the honey now dripping onto the table. He reached around, grabbing a towel from the cabinet handle beside him, and cleaned the sticky mess from his arm. Roween asked how it happened. He told her about the vines and the thorns and she sat on the table in a huff.

"I hate those vines; they choke my trees. Nothing's fine; they're full of jealousy."

"What do you mean? They're plants, too, aren't they?"

"No, they're mean, and I mean them all. They choke my trees because they grow so tall."

Ron offered to cut the vines the next time he was there and she thanked him for the offer as he finished wiping the honey from his arm before heading to the sink to wash off the rest.

Drying his arm, he turned to see them together; they seemed to be disagreeing about something.

"I must ask, and I will. It's just a task, please be still," he heard Roween tell the others.

She looked serious when he asked what this was all about. She again told him about the missing sylphs. *"The men from that dark, dark night, for me, you defended, they took fright, and it ended,"* referring to those wearing the electronic gear a few nights ago. *"I sensed they work for a magic, not happy for this world. I fear something tragic, yet still to be unfurled."*

An ominous statement from such a vibrant sprite, but then again, she might be right—great, now I'm thinking in rhyme.

Ron composed himself and asked how to start looking for clues. Josclyne was about to speak but said nothing, only returning again to a thought. Then Roween spoke. Her words were fast, as she glowed brightly, like a spark of inspiration. *"We speak with Supp, she will know; she's on the up, tomorrow we'll go."*

"Amanda? You want to speak with Amanda tomorrow?" Ron confirmed.

She nodded, then told him how Amanda had been speaking with a man, someone her mother had taken her to see to quell her rampant imagination. She told him what Amanda had said: "He is always asking about fairies and other magical creatures, and that she is to remember this is not real because fairies aren't real."

I'd have to disagree with that last statement, for obvious reasons, Ron thought. Still, it seemed like a sound plan. Since it was late, he agreed, tomorrow they'd meet with Supp.

Chapter Four

A sliver of morning sunlight made Ron open his eyes as its warmth roused him from sleep. Sitting on the edge of his bed, he looked around in the twilight illuminating the collection of his existence. It took a few moments to make himself believe he wasn't still dreaming. Although seeing the small, glowing form before him was hard to ignore.

"You're awake, you're awake. Haste you make, the day you take."

"Great, inspirational words from a fairy," Ron mumbled.

His comment was greeted without her usual humor. Seeing her displeased scowl, he almost wished he was dreaming again. Though he'd never awoken to someone so lively before, and wasn't ready for the sudden forward momentum as she pushed him out of bed. There was an audible *thump* as he landed. His sudden contact with the ground was shortened by the sudden pull on his collar, hoisting him to an unsteady standing position.

As he rubbed the sleep from his eyes, she again appeared before him. *"No time to waste, or grab a cup. The day we grace, and meet with Supp."*

He groaned silently as the sprite before him continued with words of so-called inspiration and dedication, thinking, *I wonder if she does this to the trees; it would explain why they grow fast. Probably trying to get some extra sleep.*

Lumbering into the kitchen, he put the kettle on the stove but took it off again, having forgotten to fill it with water. He splashed his face with the cold spring water to clear his head, grabbed coffee from the cupboard, and sat down, waiting for the kettle to whistle. Roween flew throughout the house the whole while. Sometimes he'd see a sudden soft flash of light from around the corner.

What is she doing? he wondered. But, before he could find out, she reappeared as the whistle called.

"Is that for tea, or maybe coffee?"

He smiled at that musical voice of hers and only nodded, still half-asleep. The next few minutes were nothing of note; a small breakfast and, after the coffee had started its work, he was ready for the day.

Last night he had agreed to take Roween to see Amanda, the young girl they'd saved in the woods several nights ago. He was still unsure what would happen when he arrived; after all, her parents had called the police on him and he was taken to jail, only to be released hours later with an apology and a fairy telling him, "Nothing's amiss."

The morning was cold; no frost, but the air had a hint of spring. Roween pulled his coat from the loose hook on the wall and handed it to him. No sooner had he put his arms in the sleeves than she flew straight into the inside pocket.

He looked down at her and she said, *"Here I'll hide, but when it's handy, when friend is spied, I'll be out and dandy."*

He gave a laugh and they headed out to see Amanda.

She didn't live far, only a mile or so away. They didn't have to drive, but he didn't feel like braving the chilly morning. When they arrived, he could see Amanda's parents were thankfully still home. Then he remembered why; it was Sunday.

He took a breath, dreading what he might face when he knocked on that door, especially since his last encounter. But they had work to do, and Roween had mentioned that Amanda was seeing a doctor to help cure her "unbridled imagination." As a writer, and he had written some fiction, to him, the world would be a dreadful place if there weren't imagination. *Is that why I can see her? Or is that why she lets me see?* he thought, then made a mental note to ask later why he could.

They reached the shiny wooden door and gave a light knock. This warranted a prod—or maybe it was a kick—to his side from a small elbow or foot. "All right, I'll knock louder," he said before giving that lacquered door a hard rap.

It opened, and he was met with a happy, "Oh, you decided to stop by. Thank you so much for bringing our daughter home safe." Amanda's mother greeted him with a joyous demeanor. Of course, he knew nothing about them, except what he had learned at the police station. They were Mr. and Mrs. Supp, also known as Jessica and Tyler. He almost felt bad about reading it from the report the sheriff had left on the desk while questioning him. He returned the greeting and after some small talk, was asked inside. After taking off his coat and placing it over the back of a chair, they continued their conversation.

It was amazing how they were acting toward him; after all, they had accused him of hurting their child, which thankfully wasn't true. *I guess Roween fixed things.* They talked for a time; he kept hoping to catch a glimmer of light, and that Roween wasn't trapped in his coat. But when he saw it move, he felt relieved.

"You know, we've been neighbors for about three years, and I don't think we ever met like this," he said.

"Well, we're only up here part-time, usually. Unfortunately, we lost the house in DC this year," Jessica told him.

"I'm sorry to hear that. I hope it wasn't serious," he replied.

They told him how they'd lost the house, how the developer wanted to build a casino, and how he pressured Tyler's firm to fire him, making it easier. The powers that be wanted the deal done, regardless of who they hurt.

He never liked when people did things like that, and explained the situation he was in as well, having lost his job at the plant some years ago. How he had spent fifteen good years there before they closed it down. That's why he took up writing; he could make his own hours.

They seemed to be nice people. She was now an accountant, and her husband was working as an international salesman. They lived in the cabin full-time, like him. As they talked, he no longer had to worry that Roween was trapped in his coat, having seen the flicker of light head up the stairs.

* * *

Roween flew up into Amanda's room, spinning around, surprised, as she saw no one. She huffed; her friend was nowhere to be seen. She glided slowly from room to room before she found Amanda sitting at the desk in her father's office, drawing. Roween entered quietly as a light breeze. She paused for a moment, seeing Jinx on the sill of the small window. She frowned—Jinx had tried to catch her the last time she was here. But then she smiled remembering how high he jumped when she used her magic to fluff his fur. Amanda told her it took hours to brush him back to almost normal.

Amanda sat quietly drawing. Roween could see the picture; it was of her tree.

"Oh no, no, no, that will not do. No, no, no, that's too big a clue."

She'd had many conversations with Amanda about not telling anyone about her tree, but why was she drawing it? She had to find out. Also, she would have some fun with her friend, maybe changing the picture at the same time.

Silently she flew to the desk, reaching her hand above the top, pulling on a pencil, making it fall to the floor. Amanda, startled by the sound, leaned over to look. Roween flew before her, waiting for her to sit up again.

As she did, Roween said, *"Mandy, Mandy, sweet as candy; she's tough and trouble, but kind and humble."* She startled Amanda, making her shriek, drawing the attention of everyone downstairs.

"Amanda, are you all right, honey?" Jessica yelled.

Ron was concerned, but then breathed a sigh of relief, realizing it was probably Roween.

"It's okay, Mom; Jinx startled me," Amanda said. Then she reprimanded him, but not really.

Roween floated there laughing, though she hadn't seen Jinx jump up on the desk behind her. As he lunged forward, ready for a treat—or so he thought—instead he found himself floating in midair, his mouth frozen open.

"Bad kitty, you're not so witty. You forget I'm tough, last time your fur I fluffed," Roween scolded him before gently pushing him to the floor. They both watched as Jinx ran from the room.

"How did you get here?" Amanda asked. Roween told her how Ron brought her here, undercover. Then she asked her about the doctor she was seeing. Amanda told her how the doctor asked her to draw the place she saw the fairy and how it would "help" her.

"No, no, no, you cannot draw. No, no, no, that plan is flawed," Roween told her. But she couldn't tell her she suspected the doctor was hunting magical creatures. She knew Amanda might try to stop him. That's why she asked Ron to keep her out of danger.

Roween had a plan. She convinced Amanda to draw the skunk's den by the river instead. When they finished, they headed downstairs, followed closely by Jinx.

* * *

When they arrived, Amanda looked at Ron with a smile, then patted the small purse she had. He figured out where Roween was pretty quickly. When he saw the picture she had, he commented on its composition. "Yes, she's very talented," her mother praised.

"I had to draw this," Amanda told Ron. She didn't seem happy about it.

Ron asked why she wasn't happy with it, and her parents told him about her "homework" and how she was seeing a doctor for her runaway imagination.

"It's always good to get help when you think something's wrong," he said, hoping it sounded sincere.

Her parents agreed, but Amanda didn't seem to like his response. He had to agree with her; after all, he did give a lift to a fairy.

He asked which doctor she was seeing, and told them he was thinking of doing an article on psychiatrists for a magazine. "Maybe I could start my research with them?"

It was amazing how easily they agreed to give him his contact information, much to the dismay of Amanda. A short while passed, and after hearing several stories, he decided to head back. But he didn't know if Roween had returned to his coat pocket. He said goodbye as he put his coat on, discreetly checking the pocket.

She wasn't there. He looked down to Amanda and asked to see her picture again. She politely handed it to him as Jinx sat nearby, staring at her purse, slowly sliding his tail back and forth.

He held her picture to her parents. "You know, she does have talent. Maybe she could be an illustrator."

He was hoping to allow Roween to fly unseen, but that didn't happen. However, Amanda was quick, and knew what he was doing. She opened her small purse, only to have her mother look down at her as she did. Ron moved the drawing to get better light, taking the attention from her. Amanda held the purse open again, hoping Roween would escape. Then, just outside his field of vision, a flash of glimmer. Then a loud *Meroowww!* and *Hisssss!* Everyone turned to see a very fluffy cat running up the stairs. It was startling, and distracting. Ron then felt a small jab into his side, followed by three more. Roween was back where she was supposed to be.

He said goodbye again, thanking them for the information, and got into his truck. Seconds after leaving, Roween emerged; she seemed happy. He told her how she was lucky the cat made noise; he didn't know how to get her back, and was surprised when she laughed.

"He wanted to ring my neck, and then he'd purr. I gave him heck, and fluffed his fur," she said, standing proudly on the steering wheel. He told her what he'd found and that he was planning on seeing the doctor to find out anything else about him. He thought an interview would be the best way, and that Roween would probably be better off away from him. She agreed; but now, they had a plan.

There's magic in words, in thoughts and dreams.

In birds and spots, even streams.

- Translated from Sylph

Chapter Five

When they arrived back at Ron's cabin, Roween quickly hid inside his pocket before heading in. After entering and closing the door, he asked why she was hiding.

She stared up at him with those questioning blue eyes. *"You did not see those hidden things? Those small and midden rings?"*

Puzzled by what she said, he had to look up the word *midden*, finally understanding it was meant to be an insult. She could tell he was perplexed, and offered a different wording, albeit very quietly.

"Those rings of glass, so small and shiny. They still harass us, small and tiny."

He was still confused but decided to look around, checking the doorway, the stones near the walk, but when he got to the tree in front of the window, he noticed something peculiar.

On the branch sat a bird. It didn't move, not even when he approached. Most animals do something when they sense a possible threat, but this one didn't. Moving closer, he inspected it carefully. It was odd, the way the feathers seemed smooth, and shone almost as if it was made from . . . "Plastic!" he said when he grabbed it.

The small black bird wasn't a real bird at all. He looked over this false feathered fiend and spotted what looked like a lens in place of one of its eyes, remembering how the glass shone on Erant's mouse head. This bird was a fake, and whoever put it there was now about to learn something about spying.

He placed the bird on the ground, covered it with leaves, then headed inside. Closing the door, he was stopped by the sight that greeted him. What had once been a simple and stark living room was now abloom with flowers and greenery. Even the ginger root drying in the cup on the window shelf was flowering.

Roween flew from his jacket, then jolted quickly around the corner. She returned moments later, happily saying, "*Everywhere, everywhere, where I flew. Everywhere, everywhere, the plants, they grew.*"

It was nice to see her happy, but his comfortable living room looked like the forest. He wanted to be upset, but seeing the happiness in her, he couldn't be. When he asked, "What happened?" she looked at him with innocent eyes.

"*I gave new life to this home of yours. It was full of rife and dust that bores.*"

It did make the place look a little better; the air smelled fresher. And he had to admit, it was nicer. When he inquired how she had done this, he wasn't angry, but she could have asked him first. She told him how life like this brings new life to everything it touches. It was an enticing philosophy, and somewhat calming, and he asked how the brownies felt about this.

She said with a smile, "*They both know, and they agree. The forest grows, and makes things happy.*"

Ron laughed, and sat on his worn couch. But then he heard Erant cursing as he moved some leaves from the shelf where he and his wife lived. "Hey, fairy, we said you could put in a few plants, not the whole forest. How's anyone supposed to walk around here?"

"Pay no mind to him, dear, he's always like this. They are beautiful," Josclyne said, and she picked a flower, breathing in its fragrance. "They liven up the place."

Ron smiled at the surreal scene, but he did agree with Erant—this was a bit too much vegetation for anything other than a greenhouse.

"Aye, it may be a bit much, but it was in time to stop those seeking entry into this house," Josclyne said.

"What are you talking about?" Ron asked.

She told him the same people from the other night were trying to get in. They were looking in the windows, seeing who, or what, was home.

"I heard one of them say they were getting readings," she told Ron.

"Readings?" he asked, before realizing they had said the same thing when he had confronted them. It started to make sense, and explained the fake bird out front.

He jumped from the couch and headed to where he kept his ghost-hunting equipment.

Erant scoffed, "You big one, they didn't get inside; we made sure of that. There's nothing missing."

"That's not what I'm looking for," he told them.

Roween flew near and was looking down into the bag when he yelled, "Found it!" pulling a small black box from within.

"What is that for?" Josclyne asked.

"They have a camera out there, and I'm betting they have others around as well," he told them.

"And what if they do?" Erant said.

43

He connected a small video screen to the box, and then the battery. He had been a ghost hunter for years, and had picked up a few tricks. The box he held was a video receiver.

"This isn't just any receiver, it is a full spectrum receiver," he said.

Roween applauded with a gleeful cheer before asking him what it did. He was ready to spout detailed technical language before realizing it probably wouldn't make sense, so instead explained, "It'll find those other cameras."

They agreed, this seemingly useless box now had great value.

It took him about an hour to find all the hidden cameras they had left behind, even a few other devices he didn't recognize. After gathering them all together, he placed them in a metal box. When Roween asked why he did that, he told her, "To stop them from working."

She flew around it. *"You will smirk, when you can't find. Ron is smarter, and friend of mine,"* she said before pounding on it with her hand. But instead of a thump, he heard her squeal in pain and watched as she pulled her hand back, cradling it gently in her other. It was glowing red as a hot nail. She flew quickly to his shoulder, where he immediately asked what was wrong.

"It's made of iron," she stated.

He was waiting for another rhyme, but she simply stared at the box. When he told her it was, she flew away from him, landing in the flowers by the sink. She took a blossom and squeezed its nectar onto her hand. The red glow faded and she turned back to him, sitting silently, wrapping her hand in a petal.

"You cannot have that in this house. It has to go," Erant said. He wasn't very nice about it.

"It's just an old box; I bought it years ago, before I came here," he told them. "Besides, it'll block the signals from those devices."

Erant had an angry look, more so than Ron had seen, and he was wondering why.

"It's made of iron; it has to go," Josclyne instructed.

"I still don't know what is the matter."

She was polite, and told him, "It's made of the one thing that can hurt all fae; it's made of iron."

His heart skipped, realizing what was happening. She was right. He remembered hearing about iron and fairies long ago; it was said to burn them. And here before them was a box of the very same. Ron quietly agreed it had to go, and he picked it up from the floor, took it outside, and placed a few heavy stones over it. He wasn't going to make things easy for whoever placed those devices to find it.

Back inside, he asked Roween if she was all right. She said she was, but something was wrong. After speaking to them, he knew they were concerned by what he'd found. He was as well. These people had placed monitoring devices around his house, and even attempted to do so inside. This was getting out of hand, and something had to be done. He spent the rest of the night thinking up questions to ask the doctor without making him suspicious. Someone had made the first move, and now it was his turn. And the doctor was a good place to start.

* * *

Morning came quicker than expected. He found the light of the sun irritating, having been up most of the night. He stretched to remove the stiffness in his back before grabbing the kettle. At the sink, he could see Roween still asleep, cradled in the flowers, her hand wrapped in petals. He felt bad about her being injured, but honestly hadn't known. He stared at that small, wondrous little fairy. She wasn't glowing. She looked like she belonged there with the flowers where she slept. He whispered, "I'm sorry, I didn't know," hoping she'd forgive him.

When he turned on the water, she opened her eyes faster than anyone could see, then flew up with a spin.

"Good morning, friend Ron, good morning, it's dawn."

She startled him with her enthusiasm, and now floated before his face.

"How is your hand?" he asked.

She unwrapped it from the white petals and held it before him, moving her fingers. She then gave a wave. *"I was injured, but now I'm gingered."*

He was happy she was feeling better.

The morning was starting early for him since he was the one first up. He had looked over his notes. Today he was hoping to get some answers, and knew he'd have to do so in town.

Reading through them again, he crossed off some questions and rewrote others. He was about to dial the phone when he looked at the clock. "It's only six thirty," he mumbled. "Probably won't like it if I call this early."

His mumbling was met with a shrug of Roween's shoulders. To her, the day was started, and that was all that was needed. Then he remembered how Amanda had told him how the doctor always asked about where she saw the fairies. That he told her he always asks children about them. It was meant to develop trust, but Ron felt it had a darker purpose.

Suddenly, he remembered about asking Roween why he could see her, and called her back from making more plants grow in the house.

"Roween, I wanted to know why I can see you, or better yet, how I *could* see you?" he asked.

Floating softly, she landed on the couch beside him. *"Your heart is warm, and you are bold. You try not to harm, or to scold. Not like the storm, or raging cold. You see the world as it unfolds."*

He looked at her with suspicion; she still hadn't answered the question.

After a sigh, she said, *"Your heart you trust, and not so wary. You are just; that's why you see this fairy."*

He was about to ask her again but she flew up and held his lips together. He even tried to move them, but she shook her head. As she stared at him with those blue eyes of hers, he started to laugh. *Guess I may never have an answer. But one thing I do know: today I will find out why the doctor is so interested in fairies.*

A home is where the world can rest.

To sleep, to love, where all is best.

- House Brownie saying.

Chapter Six

"It's good to hear your interest. I'm always willing to speak with a member of your profession, Mr. Wilt. How about I pencil you in for two o'clock?" the man said.

"Two it is, then. I look forward to our meeting, Dr. Terrell," Ron said over the phone.

The doctor hung up and wrote in his empty calendar. He always kept Wednesdays free so he could pursue his other interests. And since his plans had been delayed, hearing from Mr. Wilt was something of a godsend.

He tapped his pen on the book sharply before standing and walking to the side door of his office.

"Edward, is there any update from the new area?" he asked.

"Not yet, Ray, but we're not getting anything from the cameras now; looks like he found them."

"That's fine. I need you and your team to head out there again shortly."

The man turned his chair around to face him.

"What do you mean?"

"You heard me. I said you and the others are to head back there," the doctor said.

"Why?" Edward asked.

"Because you are going to put out new cameras and sensors, and this time, make them more difficult to find," he growled.

"That equipment's expensive. I'm not going to lose any more of it." Edward now stood, holding his ground.

The doctor skillfully pulled a wooden stick with symbols and a crystal embedded in it from his pocket and pointed it at Edward, who fell back in his chair.

"You'll do as I tell you; it's wise to remember," Dr. Terrell told him.

Edward remained silent. He had seen that look in the doctor's eyes before. It was usually followed by lightning from that wand.

"I'm disappointed by your performance recently; maybe I should find someone else to assist me," he declared, glaring down.

"How soon do you need them?" Edward asked.

"I want you out there around two, and make sure you try the house again. I went over the readings you collected and there is something there I want," Dr. Terrell ordered.

Edward stared at the wand the doctor held. He had been on the receiving end of it before, and knew what the doctor could do.

"Yeah, sure, Ray, I'll get everything set. No problem," he said before inching back as the doctor moved closer.

"That's good to hear. Also, Edward, I am a professional. Please address me as Dr. Terrell, not by my first name. You're starting to sound like when I found you and the others scrounging for work down in Texas. I pay a decent wage, don't I?"

Edward nodded, his eyes wide, staring at the man before him. "Yes, Dr. Terrell."

"That's better. Now get your equipment ready. I have a meeting with Mr. Wilt at two," he instructed as he turned to leave.

"I thought you were working with those things we captured," Edward replied.

The doctor's slow turn toward him made him feel uneasy.

"Unfortunately, they'll have to wait. I have a meeting with the man whose house you are going to. Do you understand?"

Edward nodded.

"Good. Perhaps we'll find what I'm looking for. These other creatures have little power, at best. And I have a feeling we'll find what I want in that house of his," the doctor said.

Edward carefully walked around him. He knew what would happen to him if he didn't.

The doctor looked into the polished steel mirror on the wall across from the monitors. He chuckled. "Dr. Raymond Terrell, psychologist, magic hunter, and sorcerer."

He looked into his reflection as it repeated his words, over and over. The doctor simply smiled as he whisked the wand back into his pocket. Turning to leave, he whispered, "I love that thing; it'll keep saying that for hours," and he closed the door.

* * *

Ron had time before his meeting and decided to get some grocery shopping done. He also wanted to have a look for Terrell's office. It was good having a plan in place, just in case. Besides, he'd always dealt with people, usually in a good way; how else could he convince them to allow him to "hunt ghosts"? Although he did it more for the stories instead of science, he had to admit, you had to know something about people in order to do so.

It took a short while before reaching the store, even passing Terrell's office on the way. Entering, he looked at his list; it was pretty standard: bread, milk, eggs, coffee, and so on. Until he saw "Honey" scribbled on the bottom. He hadn't written it; but seeing the flower drawn in the "o" gave him a good idea who had.

I seem to have gone through a lot of that these past few days, he thought, then smiled and headed inside.

It didn't take long for him to get everything. He was putting the bags in the trunk when he heard someone yelling into their cell phone, recognizing it as Jessica.

"Look, I'm waiting here right now. Where is the driver? I called for a tow over an hour ago."

She sounded angry. He thought about just getting in his truck and leaving, but hearing her anger turn to panic changed that.

"What do you mean, you don't have a loaner? I need one today. I have a very important errand!"

He stared at her, seeing how upset she was, and decided to help. But when he waved to her, she didn't notice. So he walked up to her and tapped her on her shoulder. "Jessica, is everything all right?"

His question was met with her hand pushing him away as she yelled louder into her phone. She wasn't paying attention, instead only focusing on her call.

"Jessica, it's Ron. Do you need any help?"

This time, she turned to see who was talking to her. She immediately grabbed his arm and held him there.

"Ron, oh good. Could I ask a favor? Could you give me a ride to the bank?"

He nodded as she held her phone to her ear.

Still animated, she spoke loudly to whoever it was on the other end. "You're right next to the bank in town, right?"

The answer must have been yes because she asked Ron again if he could drop her off there. He agreed to help, and it didn't take long before the tow driver arrived. It seemed quick the way he hooked up her car and drove away.

"Thanks so much, you're a lifesaver. I have to get to the bank, and the garage is near there so . . . I'm hoping I'm not imposing too much."

"Nah, I have to drive by there anyway to head out of town," he told her.

They got in his vehicle and followed the tow truck. Along the way, they talked. She told him about her job and how she had been working as a bookkeeper for several businesses in town. She even asked if he needed any work done. He declined with, "My books aren't difficult." And as they came upon a small bookstore named Paragon Mists, he was about to make a joke about writers making their own books when she suddenly rolled down the window and yelled "Crazy person!" at a woman wearing a scarf walking down the street.

Her actions made the woman turn in surprise, and seeing the hurt look on her face, Ron couldn't help but feel embarrassed by Jessica's actions. When she sat back, she told him who the woman was. She was the one who owned the bookstore.

"She's the one filling my daughter's head with all that magic and fantasy stuff. I think she's a witch or something." She seemed genuinely angry.

He could understand her being upset, but also, being a writer without imagination, he'd be out of a job.

"Amanda's just a child. Don't you remember believing in such things?" he said.

She faced forward. "The world's not that easy, you know that."

Unfortunately, he did, and with all honesty, he still wished he could believe that things were as magical as he once did, when he was young. Then he remembered he'd been dealing with a fairy these past few days. He must have had a perplexed look on his face, because Jessica asked him what was wrong.

He couldn't tell her the truth, so he decided to say, "Nothing, just thinking about some questions I was going to ask Dr. Terrell."

She thought for a moment before saying, "See, that's what imagination's useful for. I'm hoping the doctor can make Amanda see that."

Her statement made him feel a little uncomfortable, if not a little sad. Amanda and he had a mutual friend, and that friend wasn't going to take "you're not real" very easily. But, then again, it was probably better her mother didn't know.

When they reached the bank, he noticed her car in the lot; the tow truck had beat them there. She jumped out the door with a hurried, "Thank you," before heading inside.

Ron sat in his truck, mulling what she had done earlier, and how that woman from the bookstore must have felt. Looking at the clock, he realized he had a few hours until his meeting with Dr. Terrell. That image of the woman haunted him, and for some reason, he felt compelled to go back. So, he turned the truck around.

Chapter Seven

On his way back, he thought about what he was going to say to the woman who owned the bookstore. He never expected Amanda's mother to act the way she did. *Guess she thought she was protecting her daughter.* He could understand that. But she seemed to have something against the woman. What was it? She mentioned she said she was a witch or something, but that wouldn't make a difference, at least not to him.

After several minutes, although he may have been driving slower than usual, his mind still focused on what to say. And when he stopped at a light and spotted the sign for the shop a block or so in the distance, he felt tense. But why? He wasn't the one who'd yelled at her.

When the light changed, he hit the gas, keeping that sign in view as the shadows grew longer around him. Suddenly, out of the corner of his eye, he saw a flash. It was small, quick, and then a million things ran through his mind on what it might have been. It couldn't have been the sun; that was behind the building. Was it Roween? He thought. Then realized she was still probably at his cabin—although he really didn't know how fast or far, she could fly. Ron shook his head; he didn't have time to think about such a thing as he approached the store.

He paused after parking. He needed to take a breath before stepping out. Moments later, as he approached the large storefront window, he peered inside. He thought he saw someone move among the books, but when he looked closer, he saw nothing. Then by the door he saw a flicker, like a spark on metal, and he reached out for the handle.

Inside was like any small bookstore; shelves piled high, smelling of print and paper. There were colorful items in the windows; they made it feel comfortable. As he looked to where he thought he had seen someone through the window, he was disappointed to find no one. He turned, hoping to find any evidence of inhabitants, but instead, again, found himself focused on the sun-catchers in the window, still dim from the lack of morning sun. *I guess they're better in the afternoon.* They did make the place seem brighter, nonetheless.

He pulled a book from the shelf behind him, half hoping not to find any more surprises. Although he wouldn't have even been surprised if something had pulled the book back, given the past few days. Once he felt satisfied nothing was going to jump out and introduce itself, he returned to trying to find someone in the shop.

He turned to the raised counter, seeing some business cards for the shop next to a bell. Reaching up, he tapped the bell with minimal effort, then heard a voice.

"I'll be with you in a second; I just opened the store," the woman said.

He pulled his hand away quickly, having not expected anyone to answer so quickly. "No rush."

Moments later, a woman appeared from the back, still wearing the floral scarf over her head from earlier. *She looks attractive,* he thought.

"What can I do for you?" she asked, and pulled the scarf from her head.

When she did, it revealed something that made him forget what he was thinking. Her hair was the color of fire, and for a moment, time stopped. It made her seem even more beautiful, and he stood there staring before saying, "Hi."

She laughed, and when she did, her smile lit up the room. He was now even more apprehensive. Besides, he still hadn't come up with an apology, and remembered some old advice: "Go with what you know."

He asked if she had any magazines on ghost hunting. She politely pointed at the rack before the counter in front of him. Reaching out, he picked up the first one there. She told him there were some good articles in there about hunting ghosts. He broke away from staring at her and opened it to a random page, but when he looked down, he started to laugh. Before him was an article he had written months ago. He held it up and told her about it.

"You're the one who wrote that?" she asked.

She questioned his integrity, but when he pointed to the author's name, and said, "Yep, that's me," she believed him, and they found themselves talking again. The conversation made it feel good to be there. She even asked him questions about his other writing. He thought she was still trying to decide if he was telling the truth, and she seemed to be having fun grilling him as well. Time passed; it wasn't wasted, by any means. He found out her name was Linda, and she was from the area. She even asked him to sign a copy since he was there.

It took a moment for him to build up the courage to say why he was really there, but before he could, he was distracted when there was a small flash from behind that startled him. He watched as Linda's eyes glanced up before quickly turning back to him.

"Did you see a flash?" he asked.

Her response was something other than he expected. "No, I didn't."

She hesitated and seemed uncomfortable, as if hiding something, before she asked him to sign another copy of the magazine.

He had spent a good deal of time dealing with people, and was known to read them very well—and usually know when they're lying. And she wasn't a very good liar. Something had flashed behind him; she even looked for it.

He gathered himself, took a breath, and said, "I wanted to apologize for that woman yelling at you this morning."

He wasn't sure it sounded convincing, but when her smile faded, he realized it had.

"You were driving," she said.

He nodded. "I came to apologize; she shouldn't have done that."

He was hoping that would help; he had just met her, and honestly, it felt good to be there. What wasn't right was the fact of why he was there, and he felt bad when she sat down on the stool behind the counter, staring forward.

"Look, I don't know what happened, but I want to apologize for her actions. She didn't have any right to do that."

She seemed soothed by his words, but much quieter.

"I know this probably has to do with her daughter, Amanda—"

"You know Amanda?" she interrupted.

Ron told her he did, and how he found her in the woods.

"Is she all right?" She was concerned.

"She had been hurt, but she's all right," he replied.

Linda asked so many questions after that, he couldn't remember any of them. He told her how he found her out in the woods late at night, and how he helped her, and brought her home. Linda seemed relieved by what he said. Of course, he didn't tell her everything.

"Is that why you were driving her mother around?" she asked.

When he told her, "No, I was just helping out; her car broke down," she seemed even more relieved.

They started to talk again, and things became better as they did. She even told him jokes that Amanda had told her; they weren't very funny, but they did make you snicker. They were jokes a child would find funny. What was better was that she was smiling again.

"Have you seen her?" Linda asked.

"Yeah, recently. I was over at their home; we have a mutual friend."

He almost regretted saying "mutual friend," because she looked at him with curiosity. In fact, it felt a little uncomfortable until they heard a loud, "Tweet!"

It made them both look toward the window, where there were now several birds sitting on the sill outside, all of them looking in. He thought it strange, and turned back to her before seeing the time.

"It's twenty till two," he mumbled.

Linda asked him what he'd said, and seemed disappointed when he told her he had an appointment at two, before rushing toward the door.

He paused when he thought he heard her whisper, "A man of words, and what he's wrote. Hear the birds, and take note." But when he asked what she said, she replied, "Nothing, it's nothing. If you want to come by later, I'm usually here till eight."

He smiled and said, "All right."

As he was heading out the door, he heard her yell, "Wait!" and she rushed over, flashing one of the cards for the shop. "Just in case," she said, and placed it in his jacket pocket.

When he got into his truck, she was standing in the window of the shop. That fire-red hair of hers framed by those sun-catchers made him smile. Then, as he drove away, he realized something. *She was taller than who I thought I saw in the window when I arrived.*

Chapter Eight

Ron looked at the clock on the dashboard as he drove to the appointment; it was almost 2:00 p.m. Several minutes passed before finding a spot and leaving his truck. The air felt chilled, and he put his hands in his pockets to keep them warm. Nearing his destination, he saw Amanda and her mother leaving the bakery next to the doctor's office.

"How's the car?" he asked.

Amanda's mother wasn't in the best mood as she replied, "Did you know that a phone charger can kill a battery?"

He nodded, having had an unpleasant experience of doing so several years earlier when he was out in the middle of nowhere.

"Well, it's a new battery. We were just waiting, so we stopped in the bakery. They just finished with my car, so we're heading home." She seemed embarrassed about having left her charger plugged in.

Ron was about to say something when Amanda interrupted.

"They have the best honey-glazed donuts here; you should get some. Everyone loves them; everyone." She winked.

He smiled, trying not to laugh, immediately thinking of Roween. She did like honey, and as they walked away, he looked at the bakery, promising to stop in after his meeting.

Ron went to open the door of the doctor's office and felt a sudden chill, stopping just before his hand touched the handle.

What the?

It felt as if the door was on fire—warm, electrified—and cold, all at the same time. He carefully placed his hand over the handle, and . . . nothing. It didn't burn, or feel cold at all, at least no more than it would on a fall day. *But what stopped me from touching it?*

He didn't open the door but instead inspected it.

"Dr. Raymond Terrell, PhD, Psychologist," the sign read. To Ron, everything seemed normal. But as he pulled his other hand from his pocket, he dropped his notebook on the ground. Bending down to pick it up, his hand moved toward the door. Just then, a sudden gust of wind hit, knocking him sideways against the wall.

He felt a small shock as he lifted his notebook from the ground; it was strange, like static, but gentle as it arced from his pen in the binding. He steadied himself as he again reached for the handle; that's when he noticed a small, glowing circle right before the *PhD*. He hadn't noticed it earlier, and he stared at it for a moment.

That's not something you usually see on a doctor's door.

He now knew there was something strange about the man he was going to see today. Something in his mind was telling him to keep on guard as he let himself in and headed up the stairs.

* * *

Dr. Terrell was working on his computer. He opened a program, then clicked a button to activate something. By the door, a quiet beep told him the device there was working, and he read the values that it transmitted.

"Good, it's working as expected. Now, Mr. Wilt, let's see what you've brought me," he muttered, a grim smile gracing his face.

Knock, knock, then several more. The doctor looked at the monitor, seeing Ron knocking on the door, before yelling, "It's open, come in!"

Ron entered, but as he walked through the door, the doctor yelled for him to stop.

Terrell was looking at his monitor, reading what the sensors were transmitting; the values were nothing of interest. *There's no energy on him at all. That is strange.*

Ron stood in the doorway, confused, when the doctor asked him to come in again.

He greeted Ron with a firm handshake and offered a seat. Ron happily accepted and took out his notes. The doctor sat and asked for a moment, telling Ron he was writing a letter to a colleague.

"I just want to finish this up, do you mind?" he asked.

Ron nodded, offering him some time to finish. But as he watched, he noticed how the doctor was typing. Having worked with computers for some time, he asked Terrell what software he was using. The doctor told him—that was lucky. Ron remembered using the same while he was working at the factory. He then realized the manner in which Terrell was typing was not in sync with what he said he was doing. He now suspected Terrell was up to something else.

After the doctor finished, they talked. Ron asked several normal questions, figuring he'd hide his true queries within them. He noted that Terrell went to school in Texas, and that he had several practices before settling here. Also, he found working with people of unbridled imagination fascinating. Ron was about to ask another question when the doctor's phone rang, and he politely allowed him to answer.

It sounded like a sales call, and the doctor politely declined. Telling Ron, "Someone trying to sell me carpet cleaning services."

"I've had a lot of those recently. I usually tell them I have dirt floors," Ron joked.

It broke the tension, and as the doctor gave a few excuses he'd used himself in the past, Ron found himself looking around the room. He could see the pictures covering the walls; many appeared as if they were made by children, and he stood to get a closer look.

"I noticed you have a lot of pictures from your patients up. Is there a reason for that?" Ron asked.

"Children are full of potential, and not marred by the world. Their imagination is boundless, only inhibited by their knowledge and experience as they grow older. Also, I feel it helps determine the depth of a problem," the doctor replied.

That sounds like a canned response if ever I heard one, Ron thought before asking, "How do you discern the depth of someone's imagination?"

Terrell gave an explanation, but truthfully, Ron didn't believe a word he was saying. Instead, he continued looking around the room at the pictures; some were very lifelike and detailed.

"I've noticed there are a lot of drawings showing magical creatures; that seems odd," Ron said.

"Not at all. I find my patients do better when they have a chance to express themselves with what they think they experience. I feel it helps them," the doctor responded.

Ron looked around. "You seem to have a lot of them."

"Well, it helps my patients. It's healthy and creative for them; plus, many have a much-suppressed artistic talent. Also, it's a hobby of mine. I think the imagination of my patients can be useful for other purposes."

His answer sounded slightly sinister prompting Ron to ask, "What purposes?"

The doctor's reaction wasn't one he expected. He looked at his watch and told Ron, "I think we may have to continue this another time, Mr. Wilt. I almost forgot an appointment I have to get to."

"By all means. I don't want to keep you. How about we continue this another time," Ron replied.

He agreed, and walked Ron to the door, handing him his card. As Ron was about to turn and ask him when would be a good time, he felt the pressure of the doctor's hand on his back pushing him out. *Guess my time here today is up!* Ron thought as the door quickly closed behind him and he found himself standing in the hall holding Doctor Terrell's business card.

Ron headed down the stairs; he was by no means done with the doctor. He figured it would take a few minutes for him to head out, so Ron waited in the bakery next door. While he did, he ordered a dozen of those honey-glazed donuts Amanda had recommended.

Only a few minutes passed before he saw Terrell head to his car. Quickly, he gathered his donuts, hopped in his own vehicle, and followed him as he drove away. Stealthily, he tailed the doctor to his destination. He became a bit concerned when he realized it was the doctor's home. Parking a few houses back, he allowed him to go inside before getting out and walking down to take a look.

When he reached the house, he discovered stone pedestals that held an iron gate. The fence wasn't very high, but something was off about it. As he reached out to touch the gate, he again felt a chill. He immediately moved away, then inspected everything before him, looking for what he had seen at Terrell's office. He found what he was looking for. There, on one of the stone towers, was a small, glowing circle.

"So, this is what magic is like," Ron said.

He looked the gate over, its iron bars taunting him. There was magic protecting the doctor's house, the same as his office. Ron hadn't believed in magic till a few days ago, but this was something he'd never experienced. He didn't know much about it. Turning back to his truck, he smiled realizing he knew some people who would.

Chapter Nine

It was still light when he arrived back home with important news for everyone. The fact that the doctor was using magic was of great interest. He was hoping they would know what he might be using it for, and maybe do something about it as well. Ron suspected the doctor knew he was on to him, or, at the very least, he may have suspected that Ron knew it was the doctor who had been spying on him. Hopefully, he didn't know about the others also living in and visiting Ron's home.

He paused at the door, looking to see if another fake bird had appeared in the tree. He was disappointed seeing just a bare branch waving in the wind, but decided to walk around, just in case.

Having been satisfied by his patrol, and the fact that the metal box containing the cameras was still there, Ron headed inside.

Placing his jacket on that loose hook, he paused as it pulled away from the wall once again. He was praying it would stay in place for just one more day. Of course, he'd been saying that for the past few years, and it still hadn't fallen.

The living room was quiet—very quiet. Even the creaking of the floorboards seemed somewhat silent. Considering that the past few days he had been met with a flurry of magical beings who seemed, for now, to be missing, he immediately thought, *did they grab anyone? Were those men here? Did they take any of my new friends?* But, seeing nothing there, he headed for his bedroom.

Everything seemed normal, with the exception of no one flying, griping, or whispering. There was only the silence of his excited breathing. He was almost in a panic before noticing a leaf on the shelf waving at him. He walked over, acting as if it were something he would naturally do. Outside, he hadn't noticed any cameras or sensors, but he wasn't taking any chances.

He sat on his bed and took a book off the nearby shelf, pretending to look for something to read. He was relieved to see Erant appear in the now vacant spot. He was about to say something when Erant held his hand to his lips, motioning for Ron to be silent, then waved him to come closer.

"Ron, those men were here; they put up more of those things. They almost got in through the kitchen. Sorry for the mess. They would have if we hadn't stopped them; you've just missed them," he whispered.

The kitchen? Ron thought.

He was so focused on what he had found out, he hadn't even seen. Dropping the book on the bed, he rushed back to check. To his surprise, there were pots and shelves covering the sink, blocking the window. It looked like the entire cabinet had fallen off the wall.

He quickly inspected the window and saw it open, but just barely. He felt anger, and fear of what might have happened.

"Someone tried to break in," Ron growled.

He immediately reached into the drawer to grab a knife, not realizing he had instead pulled out a spoon, then rushed around the house.

If anyone is still here, I'll find them.

68

He found no one, but, knowing who might have been there, he grabbed that little black box and searched for signals. He found two, and they pointed inside his home.

They've gone too far, he thought.

Finding so few, however, meant he must have arrived back too early for them to finish. And as he switched to another frequency, he saw movement. The screen before him showed the ground moving beneath it.

One of their cameras is still transmitting; they must not have had a chance to turn it off.

He watched, looking for a clue to where they were, and when he saw the remains of the stone wall by the creek, he had them. Quickly, he dropped the spoon and grabbed the bat by the door. Ron always kept one there, just in case he needed it for a large animal trying to get in.

He headed out to find them.

* * *

Edward and the others were walking as quickly as they could away from the cabin. They needed to get as far as they possibly could, having almost been discovered.

"Dammit, Phil, why'd you have to park on the other side of this place?" Edward barked.

"Hey, you're the one following the doc's orders; I'm just taking the credits. Besides, it's easier to run down a road when you're breaking into someone's house. How was I supposed to know he'd come back the other way? We just have to walk around; that's all," Phil replied.

Edward looked at Grey, who was quiet. "Did you find those other cameras outside, Grey?"

"I don't know you. I'm on probation, remember? And the doc was giving me credits for this. None of you said anything about breaking and entering. I didn't sign up for this. As far as I'm concerned, I don't know any of you," Grey shot back.

"Relax. The doc's got us covered. And besides, that mess in the kitchen will keep him occupied. That shelf fell when we pushed the window in, didn't it?" Phil said.

Grey looked at him with disdain; he was only doing this job to stay out of trouble. And hopefully get some college credit. Back in Texas, he'd wrecked his car and was given a choice. Although no one was injured, the fact that he hit a judge's car made it a problem. They were lenient, but didn't want him in the state for a while, so he took the job here. As he turned to yell at Ed, a tree snagged the bag he was carrying and he toppled to the ground, spilling its contents onto the forest floor. They stopped to pick up the electronics, thinking they were far enough away to take a breather.

Edward was still hassling them about not finding the other cameras, and they started to argue, each of them blaming the others for not doing their part. And when they started shouting, they didn't notice Ron close behind them in the woods.

He readied himself to fight, holding his bat ready to strike. These men invaded his home and placed those damn cameras all around. He was ready to take them down and beat some respect into them when a flash appeared before him, making him stop.

"Ron, please, they are not of dearth, these men are not the worth," Roween said, then quickly hid behind a tree.

"What are you doing here? They'll see you!" Ron said.

"They have not seen me; they have not seen this fairy."

He couldn't believe she was stopping him. He was angry, and

wanted to teach them a lesson. So he moved closer to the tree she was hiding behind and talked to her out of sight.

"I'm doing this because they put more cameras up. They are trying to find you and the others," he said.

"I know, you are a good man. Please remember, there is a plan."

His anger subsided as she spoke. She seemed to have that effect. But he still felt these people had to pay.

"If I can't hurt them, I'm going to scare them," he said.

Roween peered around the tree, then nodded with a big smile.

"Good," Ron said, grinning.

He walked as quietly as he could toward them; the whole while, they continued to argue. They never heard him coming. He was feet away from them as they continued yelling. He was beginning to rethink his actions; they didn't seem smart enough to be criminals.

Who starts yelling while running away from a crime? These guys are idiots, Ron thought.

He leaned against a tree, deciding if he was going to do anything further to them, but when the one who seemed to be the leader called Ron a moron, he decided to scare them, just a little.

Ron readied his bat, holding it high. He took a deep breath, then ran toward them, yelling. He caught them by surprise. The leader scurried away as he focused on him, bringing the bat down on the ground before his feet. The men could see the white in his eyes glaring wide. On Ron's right he heard *phhhhhhrt*, and the sound of someone relieving themselves in their pants. The other screamed like a monkey stepping on a banana.

Ron brought the bat up again and swung, making sure he missed; after all, he did promise he'd only scare them. It took a few moments, but one of them grabbed the bag they were carrying and ran away. Ron stood watching as they disappeared into the woods.

Roween flew beside him, giving her approval of his actions, before they headed home.

* * *

A while later, Edward and the others found themselves walking in the dark, only a small flashlight lighting their way. They argued while approaching the truck.

Grey was telling Phil, "You're riding in the back. You're not getting in my truck."

They were all tired. They had been chased, and were lost for the last few hours. Edward threw the bag containing what was left of the equipment onto the seat, then he heard something.

Beep. A pause and two more. *Beep, beep.*

He grabbed the bag, recognizing the sound of the sensors. Rifling through it, he found the one that was beeping.

"It must have turned on when we dropped it," Grey said.

Edward pulled out his laptop, then plugged in the sensor. He was hoping to find out what set it off.

"The readings are off the scale; we've found something!" Edward said.

On the screen, it showed the spike in the power it detected. He then pulled the time code from the sensor. It indicated approximately three hours ago, about the time they were chased from the woods.

"We got something?" Grey asked.

"And it's about the time we ran into that guy, too," Edward shot back.

They looked at each other. "We really got something?" Phil said incredulously.

"Yes, we did. But Ray's not going to like hearing we lost most of the equipment again," Edward replied.

His statement made them all a little despondent, knowing they were probably going to have to face Dr. Ray's wrath. But, as Edward looked over the numbers, he smiled.

"It might not be a total loss. If these readings happened while he was around, that means it was either with him or close by. It's probably following him."

That was good news, and they were now hopeful the doctor wouldn't zap them when they returned. They all agreed, then got into the truck after Edward told them he had a plan to catch what the doc was looking for.

With flight and fight, to tough and tumble.

A fairy sight keeps wings luff and humble.

- A Fairy's advice for humans.

Chapter Ten

The walk back to the cabin was short, and both Ron and Roween remained quiet in case other devices were still hidden in the woods. After mentioning it was getting hard to see, Ron was surprised when his face suddenly was full of fairy dust. He asked, "What was that for?"

She shrugged her shoulders, then motioned for him to hurry. The darkness was overtaking the woods, and he hadn't realized what she had done until he opened his front door. The few lights that had been left on now blinded him with their luminance, causing him to lurch backward, like a vampire from the sunlight.

Roween flew from his pocket again, dousing him with fairy dust. "*Sorry that you can't see. That was the fault of this fairy. Your eyes are fine, you will see. We have no time, follow me.*"

His vision was returning, but still blurry. After blinking several times and attempting to wipe away the dust, which seemed to have evaporated into nothing, he felt a small hand grab the tip of his nose. A gasp escaped him as he felt her pull him forward, leading him by it. He laughed as he stumbled into the kitchen. He blinked several more times before he could see that small trickster, smiling at him, the tip of his nose still in her hand.

She released him and floated to the pile of what remained of the kitchen shelves before jumping down to close the window. She then used some of her magic, making all the windows frost over with a yellow tint. Curious, he looked closely, then touched it, and left a streak of clear glass as he dragged his finger across. It was clearly a yellow powder, and he knew what it was. He had seen this every spring; it was the bane of many people who suffer from allergies.

"You covered my windows with pollen?"

Roween nodded, a big smile on her face.

"Pollen? On the inside?"

She gave him that innocent look of hers before nodding, and said, *"Now they cannot see, or hear. Our words ring like bees on a weir."*

Weir? What's that mean again? Oh right, a small waterfall on a river, he thought, before saying, "Like buzzing, and water running—white noise?"

She thought about what Ron said, then gave him a look and her head a tilt before nodding.

"So, they won't be able to hear us at all?" he confirmed.

She nodded and flew into the living room, motioning for him to follow.

Erant and Josclyne joined them. He told them about what he had found out about the doctor. They had their theories, and all seemed to have the same conclusion: the doctor was harvesting magic.

Ron became concerned not seeing a smile on Roween; her silence and staring was unnerving. *Was something wrong?* She hadn't said anything, as of yet. There had been plenty of opportunities; the walk home, and now with everyone here.

"Aye, you said that the symbol glowed after you touched it," Erant said.

Ron told him it had, and he related the strange way he had found it, telling them, "It seemed like the wind wanted me to be careful with that door."

"That's probably why that doctor didn't sense any magic on you," Josclyne said.

Ron had to agree; of course, he didn't know anything about magic, or how it worked. And as he described how it happened again, Josclyne stopped him.

"Wait, did you say you felt a shock?"

Ron nodded.

"Where did you feel it—on your hand, on the door, or the ground?" she asked.

"The ground, but it wasn't painful. It sort of . . . let me know it was there," he replied.

"Were you holding anything in your hand?" she asked. Ron nodded. "What was it?"

He searched his pocket for his notebook, then remembered he had left it in his jacket. He pulled it from its hook and watched as the screws finally gave way and the hook fell to the floor. He picked the golden hook from the ground, and using his thumb, tried to screw it back on the wall. It stayed, but just barely.

"Ah, you big one. Fix it proper. It won't take that long," Erant grumbled.

Ron turned and hung his head in shame in agreement. *Guess it is finally time I fixed it.*

He sat down again, took his notebook from his pocket, then tossed his jacket over the arm of the couch. He showed it to them, but Roween seemed more interested in his jacket. *I still don't know what's wrong with her, but by the way she is eyeing me, something tells me I'll know soon.* She had that simple knowing smile. It wasn't smug; it was as if she was up to something.

He showed them the notebook, and opened it to read some notes. He had scribbled something, and reminded himself he had to finish what he was writing. It was a bad habit he'd had since school; it may have been poor note-taking, but it did force him to develop a good memory. He had just pulled the pen from the binding when Josclyne grabbed it.

"That's silver, isn't it?" she said, pulling it from his grasp.

They all inspected it. "Aye, it is. That's what saved you."

Ron didn't know what they were talking about, and asked them to explain.

"Silver grounds human magic," Josclyne stated.

"So, that shock I felt was my pen grounding the doctor's magic?"

Seeing them all nod in unison was somewhat strange.

"That is why you have a gift with silver. So others cannot lift, or pilfer," Roween said.

He didn't know what she was talking about at first, but remembered about her gift from the other day. He had forgotten the wooden ring; it was supposed to protect him.

He immediately regretted telling her he had forgotten. She flew over to Ron, almost choking him as she pulled his collar. When she released him, she floated nearby, her arms crossed, with an equally cross stare.

"Ah, I'll get it. You left it on that table by your bed," Erant said. He turned to see Roween glaring at Ron. "And I'd better be quick; maybe you'll still be alive when I get back," he chided.

Josclyne laughed; Roween wasn't amused.

"I'm sorry, I had other things on my mind. Can you forgive me?" Ron said with a half-hearted plea.

"Dear, you have to forgive him. Besides, if he had it on him, and that doctor found it, who knows what may have happened?" Josclyne said.

Ron followed the brownie's statement with the best pleading eyes he could muster, making his fairy friend smile.

Erant returned with the ring and the chain. He barely had the chance to speak when Roween rushed him, taking the chain and ring. She put them together, then flew over Ron's head, placing it quickly around his neck before tucking it under his shirt.

She flew over to the arm of the chair and looked him up and down before landing on his jacket. They reminded him about how silver helped against the magic of humans; Roween told him more about how her gift worked. *Apparently, I was supposed to hold onto the ring and throw it without letting go.* She again repeated, *"If you are lost, and on your own, this will help you find your true home."*

Ron repeated what she said, and looked at the small wooden ring before putting it back under his shirt. Ron listened as the fairy told him how the ring brings forth the strength you have inside. Honestly, he was still thinking about everything else that had happened today. And he almost missed Erant joking about him still being alive, having seen Roween's expression. And Erant's miming, mocking her, was funny, making everyone laugh. Suddenly, a small flash came from where Roween was, and then they heard a *clunk* as something hit the floor.

Roween flew over frantically to see what it was, knocking

Ron's jacket from the arm of the chair. The hook, which he thought had been reattached to the wall, had fallen. Roween returned holding it, looking up at him with fake sad eyes.

He took it from her. "You're right, I should fix it."

She gave a smile as he moved to the other side of the couch and pulled his jacket from the floor when something fell from one of its pockets. It was the card from Linda's shop.

"What is that, Ron?" Josclyne asked.

"Oh, it's from a shop I went to today—met a very nice woman, too," he replied.

"Well, don't keep us in suspense; tell us about her," she insisted.

He told them about the shop, and the woman; how he couldn't forget her fire-red hair. In fact, it was the one thing that resonated in his mind. And also, something that Roween had said. Not to mention the flashes of light that led him in there. Roween was unusually quiet, but that all-knowing look of hers gave her away. And when she said, "*Something red, and someplace new. New places tread, good for you,*" he knew she had something to do with it.

Ron shook the card at her. "You were in the shop, weren't you?"

She just gave him an innocent pout.

Erant looked puzzled. "What's that about?" This caused Josclyne to shake her head.

"Erant, I think they take us for fools. Roween is a fairy, now a friend, and her latest venture—matchmaker," Ron said, holding the card before him.

Erant nodded, then jumped next to Ron. "They are crafty, aren't they? Always seeming one step ahead."

He elbowed Ron, then leaned against his arm. "But we know things, don't we? Just not the same things."

Ron had to agree with him. "I'll call her, but I need to fix this hook first."

Roween clapped her hands as Josclyne gasped a happy, "Yes!"

Ron looked at Erant, who shook his head as he hopped onto Ron's shoulder to supervise. He did what he could for that brass hook. The screws didn't want to seem to hold in the wall, but for now, it was staying where it was. Ron pulled on it, and frowned when he watched it pull a bit from the wall.

"Eh, that plaster's soft. That screw won't grab onto anything," Erant said.

Ron nodded, knowing he'd have to find a way to fix the wall before that hook would sit right. He hung his jacket on it, hoping it remained off the floor. It not moving was a good sign. He turned to see Roween and Josclyne talking, but they stopped when they noticed him.

"Eh. They're up to something. Don't know if you should be worried." Erant smiled, then gave him a prod.

"How do you know they're not talking about you?" Ron said.

Erant shot him a look of intrigue, but when Roween pulled Ron down to the couch and Josclyne pushed the phone toward him, both men were sure it wasn't about Erant.

"You made a promise to this fairy; if you renege, it could get hairy. I'll make you beg."

It almost sounded like a threat, but seeing her smile, Ron knew she had something up her sleeve. He dialed Linda's number; she was surprised to hear from him so soon. There was something about her he couldn't shake from when they met. Not to mention he had figured out that Roween had also been at her shop for some other reason. He found himself a little self-conscious while they spoke, but it wasn't because of her, it was mainly because of the small ears now pressed against the phone listening.

"Eh, leave the man be. The two of you should be ashamed. Haven't you meddled enough?"

Erant's comment was met by a harsh gaze as Josclyne told him to shush. Roween flew so close, her wings, which Ron had never actually heard before, now fluttered loud enough to make it difficult to hear. But when Linda asked what that buzzing sound was, Roween pulled away quickly, taking Josclyne with her.

Ron laughed quietly, watching them tumble to the arm of the couch, and Erant said, "Eh, serves you right. Both of ya."

Ron learned she had more than just books in her store; she also had items for costumes. In fact, she told him how busy it was around Halloween. They talked for some time, and it was getting late. When he finally asked her if she was free for lunch tomorrow, Roween rushed over, grabbing onto his hand tightly, her ear to the phone, her wings silent. When she heard Linda say she was, Roween flew up, glowing, fairy dust spinning from her as she did a pirouette.

A few minutes more passed before he hung up, the whole time resisting laughing at Roween's display.

"I take it all went well, judging by the actions of these two," Erant said before his wife gave him a shove.

"I think it did," Ron replied.

Erant gave him a nod, then leaned over. "I don't think you'll have to worry about being late. I'm sure these two'll remind ya."

Josclyne shook her head. "No, we won't."

It was funny to see them so interested in this situation, but Ron became concerned again when he heard Roween mutter, "*I made a promise, one so true. So many branches, which to choose.*"

"What was that?" he asked, breaking her from thought.

"*Nothing of note, or your concern, just a mote, nothing to learn.*"

She floated away to the window with a smile as sly as a fox, and a mild feeling of terror filled him. She pulled a plant from the counter where it had landed and placed it back on the sill. With her magic, she rolled the leaves around her, and bid them all a good night. Erant and his wife did the same. It was late, and Ron was feeling the results of the day as well, so he headed to bed. Stopping in the doorway of the room, he thought he heard a whisper, and turned to see the glow by the window fade, making everything come to a soft stillness. It was calm, but he had other things to think about. After all, tomorrow was coming, and he could tell it was going to be an interesting day.

If you hear a buzzing bird, or see a honey bee.

Speak without a word, it could be a fairy.

- Words heard on the wind.

Chapter Eleven

Roween awoke as the tendril of the plant touched her cheek, and pushed the leaves from around her. She had asked it to wake her before the morning glow of dawn appeared. She had work to do, and even though she was of magic, some things are still best left to things of nature. She stretched and floated over her bed; the night still present as she stared out the window.

"A fairy's light can here be seen. I must travel light and try not to sheen," she said in a fairy whisper before she flew toward Ron's bedroom, her light dim as an unlit candle.

She flew beside him, then smiled seeing his sleeping eyes staring into dreams. But she huffed quietly and crossed her arms when she saw the ring and chain on the table next to his book. She said nothing, but instead opened his book, and taking his pen, wrote a note. Her words were those of a fairy, and not able to be read by any other, without a little help, of course. She placed the pen on the table as quiet as a breeze before taking the ring and placing it on the page. In an instant, the words turned into human words, and she stood tall before flying over to his ear.

"These words are for you, and you will see. These words are to do, so listen to me," she said in a wispy voice, making Ron shift as she spoke.

It's not known by many, but a fairy's words have a magic of their own. How else can you explain a sudden idea or thought you have? That's a fairy whispering to you.

She touched his ear, making him twitch, and floated quietly from him; she had work to do. Ron had mentioned that the wind seemed to not want him to enter the door at the doctor's office. She suspected the sylphs had found their friends, but were unable to enter due to the doctor's magic. They may have also felt the magic on him and decided to save him any trouble the spell may have caused. Roween flew from his room, then through the crack she had used earlier, and headed into town.

She flew as fast as a stormy breeze, and in no time arrived at the doctor's office. She inspected the doorway, being careful not to touch it. She had seen human magic before. It was nothing like fairy magic; it was harsh, tempered, and when it is stolen, it is cold. She looked at the door, trying to see through the darkened glass when she felt a breeze grab her wings, pulling her away from it.

"Please be careful, and do not touch, that magic stings, and hurts very much."

Roween turned, seeing a translucent sylph floating behind her.

"I would not touch that human's spell. I know human much, and very well," she responded.

Her reply was met with bewilderment as the sylph moved closer. Roween calmed her savior, although she didn't need saving. She was there to find those who helped Ron, and this sylph was a good start.

"What are you called? My name's Roween."

The sylph gave a bow as she flew. *"La-phia, I'm called, as I always have been."*

Roween then asked about the door and what she knew about the doctor's actions. She was somewhat sad as she told Roween about the others who were missing. But when Roween asked if La-phia had helped a human, she was happy to hear her response.

"Yes, a man, with magic glow, I graced his head with a blow. He touched the ground, and that made his magic go," she said, before making the wind blow hard against the door.

Roween had found the one who had stopped Ron, making him ground himself before entering. The sylph told her she was hoping to tag along with him to find out what happened and relate it to her friends, but when she felt the magic stronger inside, she turned away.

Roween then told her how they planned to work together to release the others, but couldn't, finding the doctor's magic too powerful.

Suddenly, the door opened, and three men walked through carrying several metal boxes. Then, she heard a sound; it was one she was familiar with.

Beep.

"What the?" Edward said as he closed the door.

Roween moved away fast, motioning for the sylph to follow. She knew who they were, and that they were the ones capturing the others. But the sylph didn't follow. Instead, she had seen one of her fellow sylphs in one of the boxes, and decided to free her. Roween held her voice as the sylph rushed toward them, and flinched in horror as one of the men caught her in the very same box. Roween was angry, but she also feared the things they held. She had never felt such fear before. But also, she felt something different about them; they had magic, powerful magic, protecting them now. She watched as one of them pointed a device in her direction.

"Hey, Ed, I'm getting a reading here. I think it's what the doc's looking for," one of them said.

Roween felt fear as no fairy should. She flew far up, high,

above the building that touched the now glowing sky.

"It's gone. I think it went that way," Grey said, pointing in the direction she had flown.

Roween heard him and didn't move, spying on them as they searched the sky.

"Let's leave it for now. We already have something to deliver to the doc," Edward said. "Besides, if it's the one he wants, I have something special planned to catch it anyway."

She heard him and felt a chill that made her wings shiver. She was a fairy, and strong as can be, but these men could find her. She then thought of all the creatures that had been taken, and she knew something had to be done.

"They can find me, and all others, too. I have to stop them—oh, what to do?"

She now felt the weight of the problem before her. She had to stop them—and keep her promises from before—without endangering Linda, Ron, Amanda, and any others. It was a difficult task indeed, and she flew toward the forest, and to her tree. She had been away for some time, and needed to think. She thought of Ron and Linda meeting today, and gave a sigh.

"Ron, you're on your own. Please have fun, I need to fly home." She then flew off into the air and, in a flicker of light, disappeared.

* * *

Behind the raised table, Terrell's face was lit by the misty glow of his work in the dark basement lab. He had just finishing extracting some magic from one of the creatures when he heard the bell from the front door ring. Glancing up over his glasses, he saw Edward and the others on the monitor. They were holding some cages.

"Looks like they found more," he said before looking at the exhausted creature before him. "Looks like you'll have a break after all."

The doctor held a vial and the magic it contained before him. "So little from such a creature. Maybe they've brought me something more worth my time." He then clasped the vial in his hand and walked to the monitor.

"Hello, Edward. Please bring those things to my lab; I'll buzz you in," he spoke into the speaker.

Edward opened the door as soon as he heard it unlatch, and following the doctor's command, brought them right to his lab.

Each step made the stairs creak. Grey said, "I hope we make it out alive," commenting on the condition of the old stairs. The others ignored him.

"Got some things for you, Dr. Terrell. One of them is even fresh from the office," he said.

Terrell looked at him with some suspicion. "What do you mean, from the office?"

Ed took the cage with the two sylphs, and shook it. "This one here we caught hanging out by the front door."

"That's impossible; it's protected. The spell would have driven it away," he replied.

"Well, we also had a strong reading of that other one you were looking for," Ed told him.

"Where is it?" Terrell demanded with excitement.

"Don't have it. The reading was much higher than these babies could handle," Ed said as he knocked on the metal cage. "Besides, it moved away too fast for us to track. But don't worry, I have everything ready. I'll get it next time we come across the readings."

"You'd better; I'm paying you enough. And that equipment you wanted cost a lot as well. I'd better see a return," Terrell warned before placing one of the sylphs in the mesh chamber. "It's probably best you didn't catch it, though; I'm still figuring out how I'm going to extract its power."

Then Phil looked like he wanted to say something. "What is it now?" Terrell asked.

Phil looked at him. "If we caught that at the office, and it was rushing at us, do you think they'd know what we're doing?"

They all looked at him; the doctor raised his brow. "You have a point. Perhaps I should keep things here from now on. After all, I've protected the grounds around here. Nothing magical can enter this house. Unless it's in one of those containers." He pointed to the cages now stacked neatly on the table.

He then placed a vial on top; it glowed.

"All right, let's see who you are. What is your name?"

And as he asked, a mist emanated from the bottle and the name *La-phia* appeared above her.

"Nice to meet you, La-phia. I'm sure you'll have a chance to appreciate what I'm trying to do," he told her before placing an empty vial in the same spot and activating his machine.

Phil cringed as the high-pitched screams of the sylph echoed in his ears. He felt weak now, knowing what the doctor was doing, and in his heart, he was having second thoughts.

* * *

Ron rolled out of bed. The light from the morning already lit most of the cabin. He went about his usual breakfast business, and did chores until midmorning. He was getting ready to meet Linda for lunch. He dressed a bit better than he normally did; he knew he was trying to impress her. He was looking in the mirror trying to remember how to tie his tie when he spotted Josclyne shaking her head.

"What, you don't like the tie?" he asked.

She shook her head again. "Ron, she has already seen you as you are; you should stay that way."

He smiled and tossed the tie over the chair before fixing his collar. He turned and sat on the bed, then saw a small piece of paper with a note. He grabbed it and pulled it from beneath the ring. He then saw what looked like scribbles and scratches that made no sense at all.

"I could have sworn I saw words a moment ago," he muttered.

He then picked up the ring; suddenly, the words reappeared on the paper. Startled by this, he dropped both to the floor. He reached down and fumbled on the ground to find the note and ring. He found the note first, and looked at it, seeing nothing he could read. But as he picked up the ring, the scribbles and scratches turned to words.

He looked at the ring. "Guess it works."

He read the note, and laughed at what Roween had written. "Do not leave this ring behind, for if you don't bring, to your ear I'll bind." Ron thought the small star above the *i* in *bind* was a nice touch.

"All right, I won't forget!" he yelled through the cabin as he placed it over his head.

He looked at the clock; it was almost noon. *What happened to the time?* he thought. He had agreed to meet Linda for lunch after noon and was already running late. Ron needed to hurry. He looked himself over in the mirror one last time, even asking for Jocelyn's opinion. After she had given him a "good to go," he headed to his truck.

Chapter Twelve

Linda said goodbye as she opened the door to her shop. Ron and she had spent the last few hours talking, eating, and laughing. Ron had walked her to her shop from the restaurant. They both knew she had to open the shop again after lunch, and she had spent much more time with Ron than she'd intended.

Ron, on the other hand, was free for the day. He had finished his article about the haunted woods two days before, and was still waiting for his editor to get back to him. Lunch was fun, and they both made each other smile. Linda talked about how busy her shop used to be, and how things had fallen off recently. Ron talked about the fun—and challenges—of being a writer.

Ron wanted to spend more time with her, but as they walked by Terrell's office after lunch, something briefly caught his attention. It was a sudden breeze that hit him, throwing him off balance. His stumble concerned Linda, and she asked him if he was all right. He said he was, but she looked back at him, puzzled by the wind, even noting it had been calm all day. Ron felt a bit embarrassed and made a joke. "Must've been the spicy sauce."

It made her laugh, and Ron recovered at least some of his dignity.

Then there was a flash from inside her shop; it startled her, and she jumped back.

"What's wrong?" Ron asked, rushing to make sure everything was all right.

"It's okay, it was just Row—ah, a reflection from one of the sun-catchers. It blinded me; I'm all right. It's nothing," she said.

Ron looked around, trying to see if anything, or perhaps anyone, might be hanging around. Having seen nothing, he turned to her and joked, "I thought lunch was exciting."

She gave a nervous laugh.

Then Ron felt a draft and heard someone speaking. It sounded like, *"Help us now. We're in need! No matter how, they must be freed!"*

Ron must have been listening too attentively to the fleeting words because Linda was standing before him asking if he was all right. Ron assured her he was, and was about to say something else when the door behind him opened and some people pushed past.

"Guess you have customers," Ron said.

She gave him a sheepish smile. "How about dinner tomorrow?"

"Sounds good; I know this great place just outside town."

"Not too fancy, I hope?"

Ron shook his head. "No, not really." He leaned closer, saying, "I don't take any of my clients there, if that helps. Besides, it isn't far out of town, just a few miles, and it has a great view of the lake."

She smiled, and agreed.

Ron closed the door to her shop slowly, not wanting to leave, but paused at the door. *Was she about to say "Roween"?* Ron thought. *Roween, reflection. Hmmm.*

Ron began to put things together; the flash, Linda almost saying "Roween." *She does know a lot about fairies.*

Ron was about to turn and head back into the shop when the wind picked up again and he heard, *"Help us now. We're in need! No matter how, they must be freed!"*

Ron again felt an urge to head back to Terrell's office. The wind seemed to agree, as it pushed him toward his destination.

Ron found himself standing outside Terrell's office when the door suddenly opened, making him turn and hurry away. He watched as three people exited. The first was carrying a bunch of cables that almost covered his face. The other two were wrestling with a heavy box. And when they started to argue, Ron immediately knew who they were. It was those same men from the woods; the ones who set out all those cameras.

Ron watched as the door slammed into the men carrying the box. One of them yelled, "You could have held the damn door!"

"I've got all the cables. This stuff's heavy, you know," the other replied.

Then the second man yelled over to Ron, "Hey, you, can you give us a hand?"

Ron paused, but had been ready for another shot at them since he knew who they were. But the busy street wasn't the best venue for a rematch; there were to many witnesses. Plus, they'd now know Ron had been checking the doctor's office. But, since they were distracted, Ron decided to give them a hand. He had to admit, he was taking a chance.

As Ron neared, a sudden gust of wind blew his hood over his head. He left it on and kept his head down. The first man tried to look to see under, but Ron pushed the large bundle of cables into him, making him turn away.

"You guys look like you could use a hand," Ron said.

He was still keeping his face hidden, as if he were avoiding the wind. But when he grabbed the handle of the door, he felt it sting. It was like a shock through his hand, but he still held on, pulling it open. One of them thanked him just before another breeze pushed them both into the door. It caused them to lose their grip, dropping the box to the ground. On the way down, the box broke the door handle from the inside of the frame. Remarkably, it released the handle Ron was holding as well. The surprise made him stumble backward, still holding onto it.

After a loud crash, and what sounded like wires shorting, the box started to smoke. Ron watched as the cardboard started to char and smolder before erupting in flames. Some even shot out like a blowtorch on one side. One man rushed inside and returned with an extinguisher. The other pushed Ron back.

"Get back, it might go off!" he yelled as the other tried to put it out.

Ron stood silent, his head down, watching the flames.

"Put it out; that took days to make! Everyone, get away, this thing might blow!" he yelled.

He then joined the other man standing next to Ron, and they all watched. Then a sudden gust of wind blew fiercely, swirling, and buffeted them around. The two men next to Ron fell to their knees. Ron knew it sounded strange, but the wind seemed to only affect them.

"The doc is gonna kill us!" one said.

"No, he won't," the other said, and rushed over to the now open box. He smiled as he pulled a metal frame with electronics on it from the charred cardboard.

"This is the one we need; I can rebuild it easy. We'll still catch that thing," he said before turning to Ron. "Thanks for holding the door, bud."

Ron nodded and handed him the door handle. He looked at it before shaking his head and turning back to that box.

Ron quietly said, "Looks like you've got it under control."

He nodded, saying, "We got it. Thanks."

As Ron was leaving, he looked in the truck they were loading, thankful they were still focused on the fire they'd started. Then one of them said, "Hey, that small one the doc gave us is all right." From the corner of his eyes, Ron saw him pull it from the large box, only to hear the other reply, "Good, the doc said we might need it if things get touchy." Keeping his hood up over his head, Ron walked away. There wasn't enough time to check out the doctor's office, but with what Ron had seen in the truck, he thought the doctor had decided to work elsewhere. His only concern was those boxes they still had. There was something about them, something that left him cold. And from what Roween and the others had told him, Ron knew he had to tell them about this.

* * *

As Ron entered his door, a gust of wind greeted him. It was strong enough to push him off balance, and as his feet left the floor, Ron knew something was amiss. He floated there, his head almost touching the ceiling.

"We are free, we are free, because of Ron! We are free, you heard our plea, our friendship you've won!" a chorus echoed around him.

His feet again felt the familiar tamp of the earth as the swirling air calmed. Before him now floated several dozen translucent figures. Small, all with a glittering smile to their eyes. Also, to say his heart was racing from surprise would have been an understatement. Ron tried to calm himself, but seeing these small, glass-like beings flying around his home was making that difficult. When Roween flew before him, she seemed to be having some trouble fighting the breeze these others were making.

"You were busy, and saved new friends. And all so tizzy, they'll make amends," she said, before planting a kiss on his nose.

Ron almost fell backward as several of the others followed her deed. It took a moment to regain his footing, and Ron hung his jacket on the hook, sneering as it pulled a bit from the wall. Moving toward his couch, a hysterical chuckle escaped his mouth, and as he sat, a breeze blew around him.

"I take it these are the friends you were looking for," Ron said.

Roween gave a nod and said something, but Ron couldn't hear her over the wind now howling through the living room. Ron tried to, but as she spoke, Ron heard, "Stop it, you windy, fleeting twits!"

"Ah, the unmistakable grumble of Erant," Ron said. "And how are you on this fine, breezy day?"

He gave Ron an angry look. "It's about time you got back; these things are messing this house up worse than you!"

Ron laughed, half-insulted by his remark, half in terror of what he had walked into. Erant hopped from the couch to the chair, then onto the wooden mantel. He yelled again for the sylphs to stop, but they were excited for having been freed. In fact, Ron could swear he heard the walls creaking because of their celebration. Then Erant took one of the wood figures that Ron had on the mantel and slammed it down hard as he yelled, "Enough!"

The sound of the spindle echoed like no other, and the air

became still. The sylphs now floated frozen in the air throughout the cabin. Roween politely and gently flew to some who were nearby, making sure they were all right, speaking to them as she did.

"Are they all right?" Ron asked.

"They're fine. I'll undo it when they've calmed down," Erant said, jumping back to the couch. "You are an interesting human, Ron; I don't think I've ever seen anyone so prone to attracting magic."

"What did you do?" Ron asked, looking around in awe.

"Ah, their winds were starting to damage this home. We couldn't allow that," he said, then winked.

It was the first time Ron had seen them use any power since they'd met; he was most certainly impressed, even giving him a thumbs-up for a job well done.

"Are they going to remember this?" Ron asked.

Erant gave a nod. "They will; what I did will not harm. Unless you want me to get rid of them." He then gave Ron another wink.

"No, they're just excited. They can stay."

Erant then reminded them that they needed to control themselves. His request being met by several dozen tiny heads with sparkling eyes nodding was somewhat surreal. Erant was true to his word, and after a few moments, released them. By now, all had calmed and landed on the table. The strangeness of what looked like a sea of clear heads bobbing and turning before him again made Ron wonder if he hadn't lost his senses.

Ron told them about the box he had encountered investigating the doctor. He especially focused on Roween, but as many of the sylphs cowered at his story, Roween told him she "had it covered." Ron had a hard time believing in her confidence.

For the next few hours, Ron recounted his adventure, and several of the sylphs even confirmed his story. They were the ones who had apparently asked for help, and they were also controlling the wind while Ron was there. It made him wonder, "Are all magic beings this crafty?"

It was getting late, and Ron still had work to do. He reached beside his couch and grabbed his computer from its bag. Placing it on the table before him, he turned it on. Ron gave a laugh as an article popped up upon opening the program. It was something for a magazine about the existence of Big Foot that Ron had been working on.

Looking up from the screen, Ron found himself watching Roween trying to corral the sylphs away from him. She apparently spoke to each as she pushed them out the door. Maybe thanking them. But Ron couldn't be sure because he couldn't understand the words she was using.

Returning to his computer, Ron saved the article before putting a thumb drive in to save it a second time. He had learned the hard way about computers long ago; always save important files at least twice, and not in the same place. Ron removed the drive and was about to send the files to his publisher when the phone rang.

It was Linda; she wanted to know if Ron was still up for dinner. Ron immediately said yes. They spoke for a short while; she even joked about the people Ron had seen in her store earlier, and how they were looking for something on vampires. Her rendition of how they acted, as if vampires were real, was very amusing. Ron laughed, but in the back of his mind, began to wonder.

So far, I've met several magical creatures. I sure hope vampires aren't real.

Suddenly, the flutter of Roween's wings next to his ear and

Josclyne climbing up on his shoulder brought him back from his thoughts. Having confirmed their dinner date, to the delight of his small matchmakers, Ron hung up. He then turned to see Erant standing by his computer.

"My dear husband, you should not be near that. Do you remember what happened to that loud music machine last year?" Josclyne said.

"Music machine?" Ron asked.

Ron turned his head to stare at the space where his stereo once stood, and remembered last year when it had literally blown up. It even started a fire.

She then told him that Erant was trying to see what else it could do. That information made Ron concerned about Erant's proximity to his computer. Ron was about to ask him to get back, but before he could, Erant jumped on the keyboard. The room was then filled with a horrifying buzz.

Erant pushed several keys as he said, "I don't understand how you big ones work this thing."

When Ron saw the smoke start to pour out the back, he knew it was too late.

"Eh, this thing doesn't work," Erant said.

Turning to see his wife staring angrily at him from Ron's shoulder, Erant walked off the keyboard quickly and stood as if nothing had happened. Ron shook his head as he pulled the plug from what was left of the device.

"I guess I'll have to go into town tomorrow to send these," Ron said, holding the small drive up as he fell onto the couch.

Erant told Ron he was sorry; Ron told him it was all right. After all, things happen, and from what Ron had seen recently, not much would have surprised him. Roween then landed on Ron's shoulder and patted his head in a somewhat comforting manner. Ron chuckled, thinking about his computer bursting into smoke.

"Hey, Erant, next time you are going to do something like that, let me know. I don't think you know your own strength," Ron told him.

He gave Ron a salute, then a bow, before sitting down on the table. It had been a full day, and Ron's mind returned to the box at the doctor's office. He began to worry about what was being planned for his fairy friend.

Then Ron had an idea, and asked if Erant could use his magic touch on that box. He politely told Ron, "Not even if it was in this house. It's probably made of iron."

Ron mentioned it did sound like metal when it fell to the ground. Then another thought crossed his mind. "Hey, could you use your magic on those guys if they came in here?"

Erant looked like he was thinking, then gave Ron a nod.

Ron jokingly asked if he'd ever use that magic on him. Their response was something less than amused. "Most certainly not," Josclyne growled. "We could never use such power on anyone from this home."

Ron didn't mean to upset her, but her tenacity made even Roween jump away. When Ron asked why, he finally understood her anger.

"If we use such magic against those who live here, especially if you do not deserve it, we would suffer the same fate as you, and then be cast from this home."

She then sat next to her husband. "We would also suffer the same pain as you for as long as our lives may be."

Ron felt bad about asking and said, "Then I'd just tear the house down."

She shook her head. "And what would you do with it? It would still exist, just in pieces, and we are this house. We would be suffering for a very long time indeed."

Ron had learned something new about his friends. His home was theirs, and they lived as long as even the tiniest part of it.

Ron apologized, realizing that he now knew he'd be safe there. At least these two couldn't do anything to him. All Ron had to worry about was anything else that might rear its magical head.

They told Ron there were many things humans don't know. Ron had to agree, but was wondering if they were insulting him in some way. Seeing a smile on her face confirmed his suspicion and made him laugh. "We humans think we know everything, don't we?"

Ron turned to place the drive on the table and glanced up to see them sitting on the arm of his couch. A fairy named Roween; two brownies, Erant and Josclyne; and a stray sylph that floated outside his window. Only days ago, Ron thought he was alone in this cabin, and the world seemed simple and boring. But, to his surprise, he had met new friends and incurred some very strange adventures. In all his life, Ron never would have believed such wonderful things existed. He found happiness in that moment, and hoped to experience it for some time to come.

Ron's eyes then spied the pollen-covered window and he felt the coldness of reality. There were those bent on hunting these beings, and they were moving in too close for comfort. He wondered what they had planned, and he thought of how they had mentioned that box of theirs was made to catch something powerful. Ron was trying to think of a way to help. Maybe he could destroy the box; but what about those men, and the doctor?

Ron must have been focusing too intently on Roween's plight, because she looked at him with those blue eyes of hers. She showed no fear, but she didn't seem as bold as before. That box had her worried, but she hadn't admitted it. She said she had a plan, and Ron knew something had to be done to stop them. Not to mention rescuing the others who had already been taken. Ron couldn't leave it to her alone; he had to find another way to help.

Chapter Thirteen

The sun hid behind the clouds as Ron drove into town. He hadn't slept much; his thoughts split between what he needed to send to his publisher and all manner of scenarios with last evening's events. Also, thanks to Erant's fancy footwork, Ron needed a new computer as well.

Ron brushed his hand against his shirt pocket, making sure he hadn't forgotten the drive. His mind then drifted to the device he'd witnessed yesterday at the office. Although Roween didn't show it, Ron knew she was concerned about it as well. None of them knew exactly what it did. All they knew for sure was that these men were behind the abductions of the others.

His mind snapped back as Ron saw the office store come into view. He also noticed people standing outside the diner next door as he parked his car.

Pulling the drive from his pocket, Ron entered the store. There wasn't anyone around, not this early, so he rang the small bell on the counter. In fact, Ron had to do so several times before an employee appeared from the back. He looked like he'd just woken up.

Ron told him what he wanted; he gladly took his money. He then showed Ron to a computer he could use to send his files to his editor. It only took a few keystrokes, and they were on their way.

"That's done; now, I have to get a new computer," Ron mumbled.

Removing the drive, Ron put it back in his pocket before asking the clerk about a new computer. He showed him several, but all were much more than Ron needed. The clerk was disappointed when Ron asked for the cheapest one. But, when Ron asked about insurance for it, the young man's mood suddenly improved.

Placing the new laptop in his car, Ron closed the trunk and saw Linda walking into the diner. He rushed over to say hi. They talked for a few minutes before his stomach growled, making them both laugh.

"You know, I forgot to eat breakfast," Ron said.

"I'm just heading in to get something. Want to join me?" she asked.

Ron could see the smile on her face grow as he happily said, "Yes."

* * *

"Mom, there's no milk!" Amanda yelled from the kitchen.

A groan slipped from Jessica as she turned around in her office chair. "I knew I forgot something yesterday."

She pulled herself away from the project she'd been working on. She needed a break anyway. Even though the client wanted this done by three, she still had a lot of work to do. There wasn't time to head out to the store this morning. She walked in to see Amanda holding the door of the refrigerator open, staring inside.

"Honey, it's not going to magically appear if you stare at the fridge. I forgot to get it yesterday; I'm sorry," she apologized.

Amanda gave a pout. "But I wanted that sugar cereal."

Her mother sighed before telling her, "That stuff isn't good for you." But as she looked for what else they had, she was surprised to find the refrigerator empty.

"What happened to everything we bought yesterday?" she asked.

Amanda shrugged her shoulders. Both of them had gone shopping the day before, and she was wondering what happened as well. But as she closed the door, they both found their answer.

There was a note. It read, "Cleaned the fridge like you asked, taking everything to the dump. Love you."

Jessica felt a bit angry, but she didn't want to upset Amanda. Instead, she took a breath. She was honestly happy to have someone else clean out the refrigerator for once. However, she wished he hadn't done it right after she'd gone shopping.

She looked down to see Amanda's soulful eyes and almost gave in to her daughter's heart-tugging performance before she remembered the project she was working on.

"Honey, I don't have time to go out now. I have work I need to get done," she said.

Amanda was disappointed, and gave her best pout. Even her mother wasn't immune to that, and started to wonder how she could go shopping and still complete her work. Amanda could see her mother staring back toward her office, and questioned herself if she needed to have cereal this morning. But, just as she was about to let her mother off the hook, she had an idea.

"I could go into town and pick up a few things," she said. Then thought, *Maybe stop by the bookstore, since it'll be just me.*

"Mom, I can go. That way, you don't have to stop working," she said, conveniently omitting the part about the bookstore.

Her mother gave her suggestion some thought and felt pride in her idea, but didn't say yes right away. Something about it nagged her intuition. She was about to ask a question when Amanda interrupted.

"It's only a mile or so; I'll be careful. I'll go right to the store, and then home. I promise," Amanda told her.

Her mother thought again about her suggestion, then looked back toward her office.

Amanda stared at her intently. *I can go—you can trust me. I know, I didn't say which store. I can go to the grocery store, and maybe stop in and see Linda. You're always stopping me from seeing my friend; I miss her, and wanted to talk about things. Besides, you'd never believe me about the fairy.* Amanda thought hard, like a wish, as she awaited her mother's decision.

In an instant, her wish was granted. When her mother said yes, she broke out in a quiet cheer. She had a chance to see her friend again!

Her mother handed her some money and made her repeat what she was supposed to pick up.

"Remember, pick up milk, crackers, rice in a box, and a couple cans of chicken. I'll make that casserole you like," her mother said.

Amanda nodded.

"Now, repeat what I told you." Amanda's mother looked intently at her.

"Milk, crackers, rice, and canned chicken. Got it," Amanda replied.

Her mother felt pride again at her daughter's assertiveness, but she still wanted to make sure she was safe.

"And remember, you promised to go straight there, and straight back," she said.

Amanda nodded, promising she was going to head straight back after the store. *So what if the bookstore was on the way back as well.*

Amanda now had a plan and hurriedly hopped on her bike, put on her helmet, and headed off into town. It had taken only a few minutes to reach the store, and Amanda hurried to get what she needed. After paying for everything, she put it in the basket on her bike and headed toward the bookstore.

She had only been pedaling for a few seconds when she saw Roween floating near the corner of the building. Carefully, slowly, she approached, as if she were Jinx stalking prey. Roween floated before her, seemingly unaware. Amanda tried to be as quiet as possible, remembering what Roween had done to startle her back home for fun.

But, as she neared, Roween turned to greet her with a smile *"What is up, friend named Supp?"*

"I was trying to surprise you," Amanda told her, obviously disappointed.

Roween flew closer. *"To scare this fairy, and the like abound. You need steps so airy, not stomp the ground."* Amanda was disappointed by her lack of stealth as she spoke with her fairy friend. But Roween turned and flew to the corner again, seemingly more interested in something else. Amanda wondered what it was she was looking at, and why she kept looking then pulling back, as if someone might see.

"What are you looking at?" she asked.

Roween waved for her to join her as she pointed toward two people under the bookstore's sign. She immediately pushed her bike forward before Roween stopped her.

"What are you doing?" she asked Roween.

The fairy waved her to look again, but this time Amanda could see who they were. It was Ron and Linda, and with a little magical help from Roween, she could hear them talking.

"Could we go sooner? I have a shipment coming in around five tomorrow morning and need to get in early," she heard Linda say.

"I'm free for the rest of today; I just sent my story over to my editor. How about an early dinner, then. Say, maybe three thirty?" Ron suggested.

"Maybe watch the sun set?" Linda smiled.

"A romantic, huh?" he commented.

Amanda heard them both laugh at his reply, and went to move her bike again. But suddenly the ground felt as if it were pulled from beneath her, and the window above moved closer.

"What's happening?" she cried out.

Looking down, the wheels of her bike now floated above the sidewalk. And before her fell fairy dust as Roween waved her hand.

"No, no, no, friend named Supp. You wonder why your bike is up?"

Amanda nodded, trying to force her bike back to the ground.

"You made a promise, and one you'll keep. For if you don't, your mom may weep," Roween said as she flew close.

Amanda wanted to see her friends, but now Roween was keeping her away. "But I wanted to see them!" Amanda fought again to reach the ground.

Roween landed on her shoulder. *"I have a promise that must be done; you are a friend, but not just one. Her you'll see when things are free. But for right now, just let them be."*

Amanda then floated gently to the ground. "Oh, you mean those two . . ." Amanda said. "Wait, I can help."

Roween shook her head. *"No need to worry, or to roam. We need to hurry, and get you home."*

Amanda refused, but when Roween lifted her bike from the ground again and pulled her along toward home, she stopped fighting.

"But we can help. I know we can!" Amanda tried to convince her fairy friend.

Roween shook her head. *"Things will work; that I know. I can shirk and take it slow."*

Amanda stopped fighting and allowed Roween to pull her bike along the road, only pedaling as they came to the hill before her house. But when it became too steep, she began to struggle. Roween decided to give her some help, pulling her forward. When she heard her friend cry out with laughter, she pulled her along even faster.

"Wee, fairy turbo!" Amanda cried out with a laugh.

Roween giggled, seeing Amanda happy. She had, for the moment, forgotten about the others back at the shop. And as they approached her home, Roween made a promise to stay with her for the rest of the day. She had missed spending time with her young friend and looked forward to her attention. But when Amanda asked, "What if we need to do something for them?"

Roween replied, *"There's no need to worry, all will be good. Sometimes a flurry will be as it should."*

I've never seen a ghost I didn't like.

Of course, I've never seen a ghost, yet.

- Ron Wilt

Chapter Fourteen

Ron tripped on the door as he rushed out to meet with Linda, his haste making him miss the small *tick* sound as something fell onto the wooden floor. It wasn't loud, but it was enough to get the attention of both Erant and Josclyne.

"Well, he's off," Erant said as he walked toward the door.

"Yes, he is," Josclyne said with a smile.

"Eh, you and that fairy are too involved in this conspiracy. You should let the man be."

Josclyne turned to him. "He's a good man; he deserves something special."

Erant turned, then shook his head and gave a laugh before turning his attention back to the door. As he drew near, he saw something glittering on the ground. "What is that?" he mumbled.

"What is what, dear?" Josclyne asked.

Erant was close enough to realize what it was and ran to pick it up. There in his hands was the wooden ring Roween had given Ron; the clasp of the chain had apparently come undone.

"Well, looks like no fairy magic tonight for you," Erant commented with a laugh.

But as he held it, Josclyne hurried over in fuss. "That's not good; it is supposed to be with him at all times. How else will it help him?"

Erant gave a shrug before fixing the clasp. "We'll return it to him when he gets back."

"I'll keep it safe until then," Josclyne said, pulling it quickly from him and placing it in the purse she wore. "Besides, I think it best if he gets it back as soon as he returns. Don't know how long you'd wait to tell him." She shook her finger at him.

Erant dismissed her; he'd had enough of the meddling affairs of the both of them, and wanted to let things be. He said as much as he walked toward their hole in the wall. Josclyne gave a huff, then realized what he had said before rushing beside him, disappearing into the shadows of the evening.

* * *

Linda and Ron arrived at the restaurant a little after three; thankfully, it wasn't crowded. They had their choice of tables and found one overlooking the lake.

The service was good and the food was excellent. After they finished, they went outside onto the balcony over the water. The light breeze barely disturbed the surface as the lights reflected on it from across the shore. The evening sun was setting just over the horizon, its shadows reflecting long across the docile lake.

"That's a romantic view if I ever saw one," Ron murmured.

His comment didn't go unnoticed, and she joined him in the hypnotic view before they began a leisurely stroll.

Being a writer, Ron gave his best rendition of the scene, but seemed to pause every time he saw her smile. Their walk didn't last long, and they found some benches. They seemed to have the perfect view for such a night. The sky was clear, and the stars were just starting to peek through the twilight now. There was a comfortable silence between them as they sat silently on the bench. But when she lay her head against his shoulder, it felt as if the world stopped, and Ron was a very willing partner to its beauty.

Suddenly, there was a small flash; it had come from just beneath the dock. Ron leaned forward to see what it was, and Linda did as well. His curiosity took him for a moment as Ron stood, then looked over the railing. Behind him Ron could have sworn he heard Linda say, "I like this; don't mess it up."

Ron turned to ask her what she said and saw her fiddling with that silver chain she wore around her neck. Subconsciously, Ron checked for his own, and the memento of his magical friend, only to find he didn't have it.

Have I lost it? Was that Roween looking for it in the water?

Questions raced through his mind, but when Ron focused on Linda and how beautiful she looked in the evening light, he pushed them aside.

Ron sat down just as another flicker appeared from beneath the boards. He jokingly said, "Must be a fairy," and laughed. Ron felt her tense, and the chain she wore rattled against her nails as she pulled whatever trinket she possessed tightly into her hand. Looking at her, he could see her eyes widen for a moment. But why?

If Ron had learned anything from his encounters with Linda and Roween, he suspected it was what he'd just said. Trying to defuse the moment, he commented about the flickering lights probably being fireflies. Ron felt her relax. After that, they spent the rest of their evening staring out across the water and up into the night sky. Unfortunately, time seems to move too fast when you're enjoying it, and soon they had to leave. Ron found himself wishing for that sliver of frozen time he'd felt earlier, when she first laid her head on his shoulder.

The ride back was nice; they joked and talked about their lives. She told him about her home, and how she had decorated it like a mystical realm. Ron found that enticing and told her, "I'd like to see it."

She smiled at him. "I'll show you when we get back."

* * *

Roween was flying through the forest with the dance of a happy bee. She had enjoyed her time with Amanda, and even thought of staying after she fell asleep, though she did remark on Amanda not wanting to rest, even quoting her mother, telling her, "It's a school night."

Amanda instead wanted to play, and also wanted to know more about what she was doing for Ron and Linda. But, as Amanda turned to grab some paper, Roween was ready. A little fairy magic can be a wonderful thing, especially for excited children. There was a small flash and a cloud of fairy dust. As Roween watched her friend fall happily to sleep, she said to her, *"You'll be smart when you go to school. An early start makes no fool."*

Roween chuckled as Amanda curled up, falling fast into dreams. She used her magic to make her friend happy.

She left Amanda behind, but as she flew, she gave a yawn. She may be magic, but even she needed rest. She was looking forward to her new spot by the kitchen window, but then thought about her tree and how he was probably missing her. She had been away for so long.

"I've been away, with things to do. Like winds that sway, so you'll never hew."

She convinced herself that there were things that needed to be done, but was feeling guilty about spending so much time away from him. Unlike humans, her tree lived long; so long he could remember the quiet, without people. But she knew people as well, and how they lived. She felt it her duty to help them find more within their short time, even if it meant being away from her home. But as she flew, the heaviness of guilt grew. She decided to see him, and, like a wisp, disappeared into the forest where they lived.

* * *

"Hey, Ed. You think this thing will work?" Phil asked.

Ed nodded.

Grey slammed the door of his truck, then walked toward them. "It better. I don't think the doc is gonna not fry us if it doesn't."

Ed shot a cold stare back at him.

"Hey, I'm just saying. I mean, you're stuck here. Me, if anything goes wrong, I'm out of here," Grey told him.

"Don't forget me. If you're heading down by Texas, I'd like a ride," Phil remarked.

Grey gave him a thumbs-up. Ed ignored them both, focusing on what he was doing. When he closed the lid, the box came to life, with lights and displays all showing perfect readings.

"Now that's a thing of beauty," he said.

Everything was working and already on Ron's property—they just needed to find a place close enough for it to work. But as Phil looked over the readings from last night, he discovered something in the pictures.

"You know, I don't remember that pile of leaves by the door before. You think it's something new?" Grey asked.

Ed nodded. "Yes, but do you know what else it could be?"

The others shook their heads.

Ed smiled. "I think it's the perfect place to put this baby," he said, then lightly tapped on the box, making a metallic sound.

"We could take whatever that is, and put this in its place. That way, whatever thing powerful enough comes near, it'll set it off," Grey said, agreeing with him.

Ed nodded. "Well, guys. Let's do it."

Following his lead, they walked toward the house, being as quiet as possible. Grey also kept an eye on the meter; he didn't want to meet up with whatever Terrell was hoping to capture. He did pause several times when some smaller readings made the meter jump.

They made it to the door, and having not encountered anything, cleared the leaves away from the spot. Curious, Phil opened the box they found beneath the pile. Ed tried to stop him. "You don't know what's in there!"

But he had already opened the lid, to discover the lost cameras. After exchanging the boxes, they piled leaves over the new box.

"Wait, won't they see the lights?" Phil asked.

Ed smiled as he pushed a button on the hand control, then motioned for them to follow. There was the sound of an electronic voice from it that said, "Armed," and its lights faded from the display. The smile on Ed's face told them everything they needed to know.

Chapter Fifteen

Linda laughed at Ron's joke as they pulled up to her home. It had been a good night for both, but she had to be up early for the delivery at the store. He did have some concerns seeing the doctor's house only a few blocks away as they drove there, though.

"I had fun tonight; how about you?" Linda asked.

Ron answered with a smile and nod, making her laugh.

"Struck silent, are we?"

"Hey, even a writer can be speechless. Depends on the company," he replied.

"Oh, really?" she joked.

He admitted it was really great to be with her, and they spoke for what seemed only a few minutes. But when she looked at the clock, she realized it had been almost an hour.

"I have to get some sleep; need to get up in a few hours," she said before looking disappointed.

The smile on Ron's face sank to a realization of that fact as well. He opened his door and walked around to open hers. "Oh, a gentleman," she said softly.

"A man's got to have some redeeming qualities," he replied.

He took her hand and helped her from the truck. Both were startled by the sound of her phone hitting the ground.

"Darn, I hope it didn't break," she said.

He picked it up and handed it to her. She immediately turned it on to make sure it was still working. To her surprise, it rang; the number was one she recognized.

"It's the shipping company; let me get this," she said as she answered.

Ron nodded and stood by, listening.

"What, is this a joke?"

This continued for about a minute before Linda ended her call. He could see she was puzzled.

"Anything wrong?" he asked.

She looked at him, shaking her phone in disbelief.

"They said the truck's axle is frozen."

"Guess they didn't keep up on their maintenance," he remarked.

She looked at him, still bewildered. "No, it was frozen in ice, almost nine inches thick. And it's over fifty degrees out!"

A puzzled look now infected him as they both tried to figure out how it happened. Suddenly, she looked afraid, but as she tugged on her silver chain, she seemed to relax.

Ron was still trying to figure out how that much ice could have happened. "Maybe it was a refrigerant leak or something."

"It doesn't matter. They're not going to be there in the morning, so . . ." she said, moving closer.

Ron smiled as he put his arms around her and they kissed. The feeling of her against him made the entire night shadow in comparison.

Linda led him up to the porch of her home; the heavy carved door seemed out of place. It had what looked like trees and a forest carved into its grain. Linda smiled as he stared. She told him how it was made by a friend, and how it was made to "keep her safe."

She unlocked it, but paused briefly before entering, almost as if expecting someone to be waiting. She motioned for him to follow as she walked inside. She turned on the lights and before them was a host of old and wonderful things. Shining, brilliant shades of brass and gold, with spots of silver and cherrywood.

"Wow, nice place!" Ron said as he looked around.

"Like it? It took me years to find all of these," she said, pointing around the room.

In awe, he had almost forgotten to close the door. However, as he did, his fingers ran across its carvings; there was something familiar about it. But Linda's smile drew him away as she walked down the short hallway. Entering the next room, he was greeted with wondrous carvings. It also shone with brilliant brass and silver all around them. Even the light from the chandelier danced from the crystals along it arms.

"I spoke too soon," Ron joked.

Linda laughed, and told a little story of what was displayed before him. "It took even more time to find these things than what you've seen in the hall."

* * *

"This is here, but no longer needed. So, disappear, my words be heeded." As Roween spoke, fairy dust sparkled before her.

Her tree filled with a sudden wind as magic, leaves, and dust twisted around the hollow. When it ended, the room glowed with renewed life; brighter, happier, and much cleaner.

"No longer unfit or hapless a must, just a little elbow grease and fairy dust," Roween chimed.

She looked around at the clean hollow, and within moments, a new layer of bark grew along its walls. She was surprised at how the dust and grit had gathered so quickly after she left. But then again, she had been spending more time than usual at Ron's cabin.

Looking down, she noticed that the ring of light no longer shone on the floor of her home, and with her blue eyes, she looked above to her new door.

"Where is the day, oh my, has it gone? I cannot delay, must be back before dawn," she whispered.

Floating to her door, she touched the new bark that had grown. *"Be tall and wait, such is our fate. Very soon, when all has run. This promise, I make, I'll you tell all the fun."*

Her whispered voice grew to silence, then in a wisp, she flew through her door.

Roween flew as fast as any fairy could. She had faith in Ron and Linda, and the things she had made happen for them so far, but she knew, like any fairy, that a little extra magic couldn't hurt.

When she reached his home, she could see her flower standing stately in the window. Her new friends, the brownies, had been able to do some cleaning as well, and its blossom shone like a red beacon welcoming her arrival. She slowed, then touched the door as she looked for the opening she had used before, when suddenly, beside her, there was a crackling sound. She turned to see a branch fall from the pile that hid that accursed metal box. It had obviously been disturbed.

"Stupid box, you shove your leaves," she said aloud, but paused in bewilderment. *"But those things inside cannot breathe."*

Cautious and curious, she floated nearer. When she heard a sound, she jumped back.

"Beep. Signal detected."

Her curiosity got the better of her as she heard it make noise again, and she moved closer to scold it. *"I know your trick, you beep, beep, beep. I'm too quick, so weep, weep, weep."*

Roween taunted the box as her friends opened the door to see what the noise was.

"Aye, what's all the noise? You got a bird trapped in there?" Erant chided.

Roween put her hands on her hips in annoyance as he waved for her to move away from it. Then, without warning, the lid of the box opened. From it shone a beautiful light that changed color. All of them were mesmerized by it, and Roween felt it draw her in. Her instincts told her to fly away and she started to, when she noticed Erant and Josclyne still walking toward it.

"No, my friends, you cannot see. That box is a trap meant for you and me!" she yelled, and flew to stop them. What she hadn't known is that the box had a keen electronic eye that watched for movement. As she crossed in front of it, a net sprang from within its light.

Roween felt the impact as it surrounded her. The leaves crackled beneath as it threw her onto the stone walkway that led to the house, then she felt its steel burn her arm. Thinking quickly, she grabbed a leaf that had been trapped as well and wrapped it around her to protect her from the metal. When she felt the net tighten around her, she struggled to escape.

The net must have startled Erant and Josclyne from their daze. It took only a moment for them to realize who was in the net. Erant rushed forward and grabbed hold of it, pulling with all his might, its steel burning his hands.

"You will not take her, you metal monster!" Erant proclaimed as he pulled back hard.

The steel net stretched as the box shifted from its place. He pulled it toward the walkway. It bellowed a hollow sound as it scraped the forest floor. But, as its edges snagged a rock, it again regained its winning stance, pulling him forward. His wife joined him, but she had grabbed on further up than he had, trying to release Roween. She pulled and pulled, trying to break the net that held their fairy friend. She had almost made a hole wide enough to pull Roween through when they crossed over the edge of the walkway. She reached down to grab onto Roween when her hand suddenly disappeared. She could no longer stretch the net and it sprang back to again trap their friend.

She knew the problem right away; they were house brownies, and they could only live within the house. That meant they had no power beyond that which was connected to it. She could hear Roween's screams muffled by the tightening net and again reached out to try and free her, but her arms disappeared before her. She tried again and again, moving down the net as best she could, trying to free her as Erant held on. But as he was pulled toward the edge of the stone walkway, his hands disappeared as hers had, and he was no longer able to hold the steel serpent before them. They watched as it cinched around Roween, pulling her into its light.

"What do we do?" Josclyne pleaded.

Erant rushed forward but was stopped at the edge of the stone each time. "I don't know."

He picked up a stick and swung it at the net. Although he was strong, the stick could not reach. Both of them watched as the dreaded box dragged the fairy into its depths.

In a moment of inspiration, Erant rushed into the house.

"Where are you going?" Josclyne asked.

"To call Ron; he'll be able to help her!" he yelled back.

"But you don't know how to do that!" she yelled as she followed.

Erant hopped onto the table next to that thing that rang earlier. He knew Ron spoke into it to Linda, and Josclyne watched him pull it from its cradle.

They both stared at it. "Which buttons do we push to get that big one on this thing?" he said with frustration.

"Wait; he has paper with numbers on it." She leaped onto his desk and pulled open a small box that had Ron's name on it. Inside were small cards she'd seen him give people to whom she spoke. She turned the whole box upside down and took one of the cards. A good thing about house brownies is that they have a lot of time to learn things from humans.

"Here, husband; this has the numbers we need!" she exclaimed as she landed back on the small table.

She pushed the numbers and it started to ring, but Ron did not answer. Erant asked, "Are we using this right?"

Josclyne nodded. She sometimes watched him, and knew how

long it took for a person to answer. Then Erant had another thought. "Will he be able to hear us?"

Neither of them knew the answer, but both agreed that when they heard him answer, they would yell as loud as they could, and maybe he'd hear them.

Chapter Sixteen

Edward sat staring at the screen before him as a small indicator flashed on the screen. He clicked it. What popped up on the screen were readings and a blurred picture.

"We've got something," he muttered. "Doc, Doc, we caught something!" he yelled.

Doctor Terrell rushed in; he responded with guarded excitement. "What did we get?"

Edward showed him the picture and the readings from the box. "They're off the scale. I think that's what you're looking for."

The doctor pushed him aside, reading the numbers on the screen. Suddenly, he smiled.

Edward was excited to see the doctor pleased by his results, and in his excitement, clicked on the picture to enlarge it. It instead started to flip through what the camera had seen. They both watched as the scene ran backward to when it was first activated. And in the scene before them, the capture of their prey unfolded.

"Stop. What is that?" the doctor asked, and Edward clicked on the picture again.

On the screen there wasn't just one entity, but three, and they were stronger than any he'd seen before. One was obviously captured, but the others seemed to be trying to free the third.

"There are more there?" the doctor muttered.

"It looks like it; but the trap was only set to capture one," Edward replied.

The doctor studied the readings of the other two, then told Edward to take one of the solid cages with him.

"But they need power; I don't have a battery pack for those," he told the doctor.

"Use the power in your truck; it'll be enough. Besides, if you bring them back, I'll pay extra," Terrell said as he pulled out some money and held it before Edward's face.

He smiled. "No problem, Doc. I'll have them for you as soon as I can get in there."

"Good to hear, Edward," the doctor said before pulling out his wand. "Oh, and you'd better take this." Doctor Terrell handed Edward his wand. "Just in case they give you some trouble. Those readings are high enough to worry about. Besides, I want their power; I don't care what happens after that."

Edward took the wand and picked up the phone to call the others; they also had to confirm that Ron wasn't at home. But as he placed the wand into his pocket, he felt a sudden strength. He began to wonder if he had to wait for Ron not to be home. It was a strange feeling, almost as if there was power enticing him. And as he patted his pocket to confirm the wand was there, he began to understand what the doctor saw in these creatures.

It didn't take long for Edward to collect Phil and Grey before they drove to Ron's house to collect the trap. They made sure to be stealthy, just in case he was home.

"So, you caught something for the doc?" Grey asked.

Edward nodded.

"It's probably a squirrel," Phil said snidely.

Ed wasn't amused and exited the truck, but paused briefly as Grey slammed the door shut.

"What part of being quiet didn't you understand?" he asked the other two.

Both shrugged their shoulders and followed Edward's lead. They quietly walked up toward the front door and carefully inspected the box.

"Looks intact. Let's take it back to the truck. Then we can see if we can get those others," he said.

Their voices hadn't gone unnoticed by the brownies, and within moments, they were at the door staring at the three men. Edward stared back at them and reached into his jacket to pull out the wand the doctor had given him. Then Erant noticed one of them on the walkway.

Within a half of a blink, Grey found himself off the ground and the air rushed around his ears. He suddenly felt something hard hit his leg as he fell on his back, stunning him. He regained his senses as he heard Phil saying, "Get off me!"

It took him a moment to realize Erant had thrown him into the others to stop them from taking the box. As all three of them scrambled to their feet, he could swear he heard something crack behind them. They found themselves looking back into small, angry eyes. Phil and Grey were ready to run, but Edward stood his ground, box in one hand, wand in the other.

"Come on, let's go!" Phil pleaded. "We don't get paid enough for this stuff!"

Edward stood firm and motioned for the brownies to attack him. But they didn't, and that was interesting. *Why aren't they attacking me? I am holding the box.*

Then he noticed neither of the small creatures had moved beyond the edge of the walkway. He had been working for the doctor for some time, and remembered something about house spirits. He never believed in this sort of thing before, but here he was, staring into their small, dark eyes filled with fire. He remembered what Doctor Terrell had told him. "House spirits cannot move beyond the house."

"Hey, guys, let's think this over for a moment. Why haven't they attacked us out here?" Edward said.

Phil and Grey didn't really care and still wanted to leave. But as Edward moved forward, the brownies never moved. And with a smile, Edward proclaimed, "They can't hurt us out here."

This brought confusion to the other two and Edward had to explain. "They're house spirits. They can't move beyond the house. As long as we don't connect with the house or the walkway, we'll be safe."

Edward now had a fresh dose of bravado as he aimed the wand at them on the walkway. He willed the power from the wand and suddenly the woods were filled with bright light as it released its force against them.

However, they were able to dodge his attack.

"That's powerful human magic, my husband; we have to be careful," Josclyne said.

Erant nodded and they moved apart, making them harder to hit. Edward found a new enjoyment in the power he now wielded and fired again, missing them both. But as with all power, its user can sometimes become careless, and as he fired again it ricocheted from the walkway, hitting a small tree. Within moments, the tree started to fall. Edward fired several times, not stopping until the tree had fallen before them all. Then, as it crashed to the ground, its top crossed the walkway.

Within moments a smile appeared on Erant's face as he quickly grabbed the tree, throwing it, trunk and all, toward them. Unfortunately, they were protected by other trees standing before them. The impact was enough to knock Grey down, however.

Edward fired again and again, one blast barely missing Erant. He was getting the hang of using the wand, and as he guided its attack, they had to protect themselves. To do so, Erant and Josclyne ran into the house, closing the door behind them. Inside, they knew they could be protected. Edward, however, continued his attack. But as the energy hit the door, it was deflected.

"Ah. It's some kind of shielding," Edward grumbled in frustration.

Grey looked at him as if he were insane. Phil grabbed him and pleaded, "Let's get out of here!"

Edward still wanted to fight, but realized Phil had a point. These creatures weren't going anywhere, and they had what the doctor wanted. They quickly packed up the box with Roween and headed back to the doctor's office.

* * *

Ron stood in awe as she gently pulled him along to the mirror she'd mentioned during dinner. It was old, with a silver inlay of fine carvings. It seemed to depict animals and the forest. He looked closer, but glare from the lamp above made it difficult to see what else it showed. He walked backward to get a better view when his phone suddenly rang.

"Do you need to get that?" she asked.

"Probably my editor," he said, pulling it from his coat.

He was about to turn it off when he saw something disturbing; the number on the screen wasn't his editor, it was from his home.

"That's my home number," he said.

Both were concerned as he answered the call, but after several hellos, all they heard were nothing but taps and squeaks. He was confused, but then a sudden dread filled him.

"I'm sorry, I should check this out. I think someone broke into my house," he said, obviously concerned.

"I'm coming with you," Linda insisted.

Ron tried several times to stop her, but when she picked up a large wooden club, somewhat heavier than a bat, he changed his mind. As they opened the door, a sudden wind blew past them. That wasn't the strange part. On the wind they both heard the words, *"Friends in much trouble, fly home on the double!"*

They looked at each other, and Ron asked, "Did you just hear . . ." His voice trailed off in disbelief. She nodded, then they ran out to the truck, leaving her front door wide open. As the lights from his vehicle passed over the front of the house, the door started to close all on its own. And as the heavy latch locked tight, above the door, a glowing word, "safe," hung in the air before it.

Ron and Linda drove as fast as they could back to Ron's home. She tried to call his house several times, but each and every time there was just loud clicking and scraping.

"Still no answer. Maybe we should call the police," Linda said.

Ron almost said yes, but with the week he'd been having, they'd probably find Sasquatch sitting on his couch, watching TV with the others.

Chapter Seventeen

Linda held his phone up and heard scratches and squeaks on it before switching it to the speaker. After the scratching and thumping and squeaks, they suddenly heard voices.

They couldn't make out every word, but Ron recognized one of them from Terrell's office and the woods.

"It sounds like those guys from the woods the other night. The ones looking for—" Ron stopped mid-sentence.

"What were they looking for?" Linda asked.

Ron continued to drive as he shook his head. "They were chasing something on my property. I didn't want them hurting themselves and blaming me for their actions."

Linda turned forward; she knew he was hiding something. But they had a bigger concern. Someone had broken into his house. So she didn't press the issue.

When they arrived, the lights were on inside and the front door was closed. He asked Linda to stay in the car as he headed in, and with keys in hand, he flung open the door, ready for a fight. He hadn't even noticed Linda close behind him carrying her bat. She entered the doorway and felt something familiar. She watched as Ron looked around, seeing if anything was missing or out of place. But as he moved closer to his worn couch, two small figures suddenly jumped onto him, knocking him onto his back.

They yelled and spoke quickly; he could barely understand them, but as he heard, "They captured Roween!" he took notice.

"They caught her?" His voice showing disbelief.

Suddenly everyone went silent as Linda stood staring at them. Ron looked up at her and was about to say something, but she spoke first.

"You're not fairies," she said, looking around as if searching for someone else.

Ron paused, trying to understand why she wasn't screaming in terror at the two small people who now stood on his chest. He stood as Josclyne and Erant jumped to the table. Within seconds, Linda had crouched down to introduce herself.

"Hi, I'm Linda," she said, reaching out her finger as if to shake their hands.

Ron stood dumbfounded by her actions, but as Josclyne shook Linda's finger and introduced herself and Erant, things became even more strange.

"I should explain," Ron said, but Linda smiled. She then pulled out her chain and produced the elegant wooden ring.

Josclyne jumped onto her shoulder, asking to examine it. She then looked at her husband. "That's a fairy ring, all right." She jumped onto Ron's shoulder, pulling the ring Roween had given him from her satchel. "You big one, you dropped this before you left."

Linda leaned forward as Josclyne threw the chain over his head. "So that's who they were looking for."

Ron furrowed his eyes, looking at her with suspicion. "Looking for who?"

"The one who gave you that," she answered as she reached out to touch the delicate wooden ring he now wore.

As she touched it, the wood gave a soft glow that moved like wispy fire. She looked at her own, and it had the same glow, as though they were matched.

Ron looked down, seeing the strange effect, and wondered what it meant. But they were interrupted by Erant yelling, "They captured that damn fairy, you big one!" and Linda released the one he wore.

"Right, how long ago?" Ron asked.

"Not long, you just missed them," Josclyne said. "They took that metal box she was pulled into."

"The box with the cameras?" Ron asked.

"No. It was different; they switched them," Erant told them.

"Switched? What was the new box?" Ron asked.

Erant and Josclyne told them of the colorful lights and how Roween stopped them from being captured by the net. And how they tried to release her, even as it burned them.

"Here, let me see that," Linda said, asking to see the burns on their hands.

Linda then took off her chain and held it over their hands. Within moments, both were healed.

"The ring she gave you has the power to heal," Josclyne said.

Linda smiled. "Yeah, I'm always using it on paper cuts in the store."

After a laugh, they told how the box and those men had gotten the better of their efforts. They could only watch helplessly as

Roween was dragged into the metal trap. Even though they had fought with the men, they were only able to attack anything that touched the home.

"That's right; house spirits can only work within the home. They may try, but anything they can influence must be connected to the house." Ron looked at Linda in disbelief of her knowledge, and she responded with, "What? I was friends with her before you were. She likes to talk."

Ron nodded in agreement; there was something about that little fairy that made you want to listen.

"All right, they are probably heading back to that doctor's office. We can catch them there," Ron said.

"You'll do no such thing. Those men have powerful human magic protecting them," Josclyne said.

"That's right. The big ones nearly singed my coat," Erant added.

Linda looked at them with disbelief. "I thought only magic could use magic? What kind of magic did they have?"

Erant stood back and pointed at Ron. "It was like this," he said, as lightning flew from his hand toward Ron. But as the spark neared, the ring he wore glowed, and the lightning dissipated before him.

"What was that?" he asked with wide eyes as Erant gave his hand a curious look.

Ron gave a sigh of relief before saying, "Glad you stopped before it hit me."

Erant looked at him and sent another spark at him, and it dissipated the same as the previous one.

Josclyne then said with joy, "It is a shield! You have the power of protection."

After a few moments of silence and astonishment, Ron slammed his hand on the table.

"Right! I've got some shield, and she can heal. We have a missing fairy, and we know where she probably is. So, what do we do now?"

Erant turned away as if thinking while Josclyne asked, "Who do you call for missing people?"

Ron answered, "Usually the police. But I don't think they will believe us if we start talking about a fairy in trouble."

And just as Linda agreed, Erant turned around and said, "I know how we can get that fairy back."

He explained how they could use their rings to protect themselves and that if that doctor were a coward like those other men, it should be easy. He even commented that Linda could hit them with the large stick she carried. She didn't have the heart to tell them that she had never used it before to hit anyone. But his plan had merit, and they went over the details to save their friend.

* * *

The numbers on the clock read 2:41a.m. as Amanda opened her eyes. She called out softly, "Roween? Roween?" expecting to hear her friend reply. But there was no answer.

Amanda sat up in her bed, looking around. She straightened the light jacket she had put on when Roween was there. Her friend was nowhere to be found. "She promised she would stay."

Amanda felt disappointed, but as she looked at the clock, which now read 2:43 a.m. she had a thought.

Maybe she's at the shop with Linda.

Amanda remembered overhearing that Linda would be there around 3:00 a.m. for a delivery and that she would be there for the entire morning. She quickly hopped out of bed and was about to put on some clothes, but realized she was still dressed from earlier. Quickly grabbing a flashlight and her helmet and quietly walking downstairs into the garage where she kept her bike, she quietly opened the side door. Amanda had done this many times before; it was how she was able to sneak out and see Roween in the forest. And just before she closed the door to ride out and see her friends, the fairy sticker on her bike reflected the light above the door as she closed it. Amanda put on her helmet and followed the light to mount her bike, then headed off to see if she could find Roween and maybe see Linda.

Chapter Eighteen

As Edward turned the corner, they saw a girl on a bicycle. "Damn kid is out way too late—she's gonna get herself killed." Just as he spoke, Roween's voice rang out from the box. "*If you harm a child, my wrath won't be warm or mild!*"

The girl had stopped at the corner and allowed the truck to pass by safely; she knew how to watch her surroundings. As they drove away, she swore she heard Roween yelling.

"Was that Roween?" Amanda asked out loud. Then she heard the words, "*You'd better let me go . . .*" She was sure it was her friend.

"Roween's in trouble; I've gotta help her!" she said as she followed the truck.

Within moments, they neared the doctor's home, and as Edward pulled into the driveway, the others quickly went to unload the prize they carried. As they moved the box, a tiny voice yelled loudly from within: "*You'd better let me go, or trouble you will know!*"

Roween's words still sang with rhyme, but their intent was felt. It even made them freeze in their steps. But Edward reminded them that the creature was sealed in iron. "It can't harm us." They quickly returned to unloading the truck.

Just outside the fence and hedge, the reflectors on Amanda's helmet glowed. She immediately stopped and quietly hid behind the wall. She could hear the tiny voice yelling for them to let her go as they disappeared into the house. Amanda walked to the gate.

"What do I do? I don't think the police will believe me if I call them saying they have my friend, who's a fairy. Think, think, who can I get to help?" Amanda asked herself.

Then she thought of Linda—she could help, or maybe at least knew who could. As she got onto her bike and started to pedal, her cuff became stuck in the chain. It threw her off balance and she put her hand on the gate to steady herself. As she looked down at the snagged cuff, she didn't see the small symbol glowing on the gate.

Inside, the little light that the magic detector was connected to started blinking. It got the attention of the doctor, who was about to run up to meet Edward with his latest prize but was surprised to see him heading down the stairs with the metal box.

"Hey, Doc, I have something for you," Edward said with some satisfaction.

"You have it?" the doctor asked with the joy of a child getting a new toy.

He quickly took the box and moved it to the table so he could extract the creature's magic. The box had a small door that he connected to a metal hose leading to a glass-like chamber, a metal mesh covering it completely on the inside. Roween saw a light and quickly raced to it, only to be trapped within the mesh and glass chamber. She pounded the fine mesh, and it burned just as the net and box had before. She was stuck; but at least she could now see who had caught her.

She could see the man who glowed of stolen magic before her. He pointed a device at her and said, "This is the one I've been looking for."

Roween scowled at him as she floated within the chamber.

"You've done some good work, Edward. I'll pay you that bonus. But first, please check outside and see if something is lurking around. Something has set off the detector."

Edward and the others headed back outside as Edward pulled the wand from his pocket. Grey held one of the magic detectors and pointed toward the gate. They approached something moving there and noticed the same girl as before—the one with the bike. Grey walked back while Edward watched her, tightly holding the wand. Phil relayed the message to the doctor.

"Then bring her in!" the doctor ordered.

"She's just a little girl." Phil refused.

"Nonsense, she has magic, and I'll relieve her of it as well," the doctor said while examining the creature in the glass chamber.

Grey relayed the message to Edward, who also refused. Just as Phil had said, they told the doctor that they wouldn't grab a little girl.

The doctor said a few words, and within moments, the wand in Ed's hands started to pull him forward. A beam of sparkling light shone from its tip, and as he approached the gate, it lifted Amanda from the ground. Amanda tried to scream, but she could not move or open her mouth. Edward felt himself being pulled backward by the wand as it carried him and Amanda toward the doctor's house. He tried to resist, but it brought them downstairs, where the doctor only looked at her and said, "You saved me the trouble of bringing you to my office. If it weren't for you, I would have never found a creature such as this." He lightly draped a rope over Amanda's hands. With a little magic, the rope tied itself together. Roween could see her friend was now also a prisoner of the doctor.

"No, Friend Supp, this is not done. With you tied up, I cannot run!" Roween muttered quietly.

She could see the doctor and heard how he would take the magic she had as well. But she shivered when the doctor said, "I've never tried it on humans before; I don't think it'll kill you. But then again, I can't have you telling anyone about this either."

Edward pointed the wand at the doctor. "I won't be a part of this, Doc. This is murder."

The doctor muttered a few words and Edward's hand seared with pain, making him drop the wand.

"You forget, Edward; you work for me. If you don't get those other creatures you found, I'll extract the magic from you instead." The doctor's eyes seemed to flare with fire as he spoke. Something had changed. The power he sought was now within his grasp, and the magic seemed to drive the doctor to only want more. Edward again voiced his opinion, and the doctor used the wand to send a bolt of electricity at his servant's feet. "You will do as you're told."

The doctor then aimed the wand at the others. "Remember, I can find you anywhere. If you all don't bring back those other creatures, I will use you as my next source of magic energy," he commanded.

The three sheepishly grabbed the other trap and a long power cord to run from the truck and headed outside. Amanda screamed, and the doctor merely pointed to her and a small cloth covered her mouth. "If you're quiet, I may let you go," the doctor said as he turned on the extraction machine to take the energy that Roween possessed.

Instantly Roween felt weak, but she resisted. She was a fairy, and not like any creature that he had held before, and her magic was old and powerful. She could resist and she did so, to the doctor's lament.

"You're a stubborn one, aren't you." He smiled. "Guess I'll have to keep trying."

He turned the machine on again and worked the dials to see if he could extract her power. The lab lit with flashes of light. As he used some sparks to shock Roween, both the light and her screams filled the night.

"Is he torturing the girl?" Phil asked.

"No, that's the thing we brought him screaming," Edward said as he closed the truck door. "So, get in."

"But what about the girl? What's he going to do to her?" Grey demanded, sounding angry.

"There's nothing we can do for either of them," Edward said.

"No way. There is no way I'm leaving that little girl in there with him," Grey said as he pushed Phil aside and ran into the house. Seconds later, Grey flew from the doorway, smoke and sparks coming from his body. They watched as he turned over, his muscles twitching as he tried to crawl away, only to be encased with a similar energy as the doctor had used to capture Amanda.

"Grey!" Phil yelled.

"It's no use, you'll wind up like him," Edward said.

"You're going to leave him?" Phil asked incredulously.

"No, we need some help. Maybe if that guy can control that small creature, maybe he can stand up to the doc."

Phil agreed and hopped in the truck. They felt sorry for leaving Grey there in the yard, but for now, they needed to find a way to stop the doctor from what he was about to do. "Don't worry, Grey; we're going to see if that guy can help us!" he yelled from the window as they drove off.

What they hadn't seen was the sylphs above them listening from the large oak tree next door. Along the breeze they hadn't heard, *"They have our friends; we need help soon, before their ends by the hands of loons."*

* * *

"Okay, how about this? After we make sure there is someone there, I'll break in the door and start yelling for help as if there has been an accident. When they come to look, I'll rush in acting crazy. While they are chasing me, Linda can look for Roween," Ron said.

"No, that's not a good plan. They said these people have magic that can kill!" Linda argued.

"Then how are we supposed to help her?" Ron asked.

"I don't know, but we need to find her soon. There is no telling what those humans will do to her," Josclyne said.

"It doesn't matter; we'll figure out something. Let's head out and see what we can find," Ron said.

Linda followed him and they got into his truck. As they drove off, Josclyne turned to her husband.

"Do you think they'll save her?"

Erant stared forward. "I hope so." His demeanor was solemn, not his usual snide commentary. She knew he was worried as well.

They stopped by Linda's house to pick up a first aid kit, just in case. As they drove toward town, the lights from Ron's truck reflected off of something. Linda noticed it and looked closely at what it was. "Stop!" she yelled. "Stop the car; that's Amanda's bike!"

The tires screeched as he stomped on the brakes, hard.

"Are you sure?" he asked.

"Yes, I gave her that sticker from my shop. I had to special-order it for her," she said as she opened her door.

Quickly, she ran to the bike lying on the ground. Within seconds, she heard a high-pitched scream. Ron had joined her and heard it as well.

"What is that? It doesn't sound human!" she noted.

Then they looked at each other and said at the same time, "Roween."

Ron looked at the lights coming from the house. As he was about to touch the gate, he realized where they were.

"This is the doctor's house; I've been here before," he told her.

"If Amanda's bike is here, that means—" Linda said, but Ron finished her sentence.

"Yeah, she's here, too. I swear that girl can get into so much trouble. If that doctor is involved, we have to stop him."

He was about to open the gate before a wind blew him back. On the breeze, he heard, "*Magic gate, do not touch. He'll be irate, and make you smutch.*"

Looking around, he finally realized what they said, but then mumbled, "Do all of you have to be so cryptic?"

Linda again said they should call the police.

"I agree, but we have to find Roween first. If they ask what we were doing here, we'll just tell them we came across the bike while heading into town."

Linda shook her head and pushed him aside, but he grabbed onto her. "Wait. The doctor's office had a magic-detecting defense when I visited. I'll bet this has the same."

She looked at the entry. "Then how are we going to get in?"

Ron smiled, looking at it as well. "Easy." He took a few steps back before running and jumping over the low gate.

Linda smiled as she walked up to the gate and he lifted her over. "I'm impressed. Not many people can jump that high."

They both smiled as Ron told her, "Used to do that to get in and out of yards while I was in the city."

"Really? Why did you have to do that?" Linda gave a mischievous grin.

Ron wanted to tell her, but as they heard another scream from the house, all he said was, "Later; we have work to do."

Chapter Nineteen

They looked around the house to see where the light was coming from and found a window in the basement.

"Here," Linda said as they crouched down to see inside.

They saw lab equipment. Most of it seemed to be glowing. The doctor stood at a control box, and when he turned the dials, a glass chamber lit dimly. As it did, they again heard screams, and the doctor saying, "You are a stubborn creature, but I will have your power."

As they moved to look at the chamber, they spotted Amanda tied up behind the doctor. Moments later, he turned to look at Amanda and picked up a long, thin device that emitted sparks.

"I used this to subdue my first creatures," he said, pointing it at Amanda. Pushing a button made an arc jump between its tines. He turned to Roween. "Since you are being difficult, maybe I'll just start working on extracting the power from the girl instead."

"Look! There she is; he has her tied up!" Linda said in a panic.

"This is not right. Call the police." She dialed her phone as Ron worked on getting the window open. With Roween screaming, the doctor never heard Ron break the glass. After unlocking the window, he realized he wouldn't fit through.

Linda had stepped away and was telling the police the address. In the background they could hear the screams, and immediately told her they were on the way. But as the doctor again threatened Amanda, and Linda saw Ron trying to fit through the window, she went to help, dropping the phone. Thankfully it remained connected to the police, who could hear everything.

"Dammit, I can't get in!" Ron exclaimed. "How the hell are we going to get her out of there? He's going to kill her."

"I can fit," Linda said. "Ron, you have to let me go in there."

Ron shook his head. "But you wouldn't stand a chance against him. I'm going to the front door. Maybe I can break in."

Ron quickly brushed by her as she looked into the open window. She had forgotten about her phone, but the police were still listening. Ron paused briefly upon seeing the unconscious man on the porch, but he had another mission. He would have to wait till the police got there.

Linda heard Ron pound on the front door so hard that the whole building shook. That got the attention of the doctor, who looked up the stairs to see what was happening. Linda took her chance and climbed in through the window.

The doctor headed up the stairs, and she ran over to free Amanda. She tried to untie her, but the rope would re-tie itself again every time. Then she heard Roween say weakly, *Use your ring to . . . untie . . . that . . . thing . . .*

Linda pulled out her ring and touched it to the rope. It relaxed. She removed the gag Dr. Terrell had put on Amanda and the girl immediately threw her arms around her.

"It's all right, we'll get you out of here," she comforted Amanda.

But she spoke too soon. Within seconds, they heard someone running down the stairs. She held up the bat she'd brought with her, but was relieved when she saw it was Ron.

"Amanda!" he yelled.

"We're here!" Linda shouted back as Amanda held onto her tightly.

Ron looked over at them and motioned for them to follow him up the stairs, but they were too late, and the doctor now blocked their way.

"You are not going to take my prize, nor that girl. Their power is mine!" the doctor growled.

"No way," Ron said as he rushed the doctor, but was stopped when the doctor used his wand to shoot lightning at him.

Ron felt the hardness of the wall behind him as he hit. He was stunned, but otherwise unharmed. The doctor could see the glow from the ring on the chain around his neck.

"You have power, too; I'm going to enjoy taking it from you!" the doctor yelled as he again fired.

This time Ron was thrown back farther, landing near Linda. The doctor laughed maniacally. "I have more power to take than I know what to do with!"

His voice echoed through the house—and outside, where it was recorded.

"You're not going to hurt anyone, Doc," Ron said as he picked up the bat Linda had dropped.

Ron swung wildly as he rushed the doctor, dodging every bolt fired toward him. Ron wasn't going down, but as the doctor fired at his feet, Ron lost his balance and the bat was thrown from his grip breaking several of the glass chambers around him— including the one containing Roween. As the glass shattered, the magic poured out all around. The room filled with light of all colors. It also filled with warmth, before a cold chill fell around them. The doctor stood in disbelief as the energy collected around his feet. The wand he held suddenly glowed brightly and he felt it wrestling away from his grip. He fought to hold it until the glow engulfed him. Ron heard the doctor mutter quietly, "So much power . . ."

The doctor's expression turned to one of being stunned before saying, "What have you done? Do you know how many things I had to destroy to get that power?" The anger in his voice echoed ominously as he tried to fire his wand toward him. But the infusion of energy made the wand too powerful for the doctor to control. He was thrown off balance, making the energy hit some of the chambers along the wall. Several burst, and the gas they contained escaped, mixing with the sparks, setting the room ablaze. Ron quickly grabbed Linda and Amanda to shield them while the doctor tried to put out the fire now scorching his arm.

"My research! My power! No, I have to save this!" Terrell said over and over.

The distraction was the opportunity they needed to escape, and Ron quickly pulled Amanda and Linda up the stairs. As they exited through the broken door, Ron stopped looking back.

"What are you waiting for?" Linda yelled.

"Get her to safety; your house! I can't let him die in there!" Ron replied.

She now understood why the ring Roween had given him had the power it did. She could see the man before her as he truly was—the shield, the protector—as was his ring. She nodded, taking Amanda away with her.

Ron headed back inside, where he saw the doctor hanging in the air. His eyes were wide and his mouth open, like he was screaming to be let go. Before him floated a small light. He instantly knew it was Roween. But her light now shone much brighter than it had before, dwarfing the glow of the flames around them.

"You thought you had my wings in fear. I'll show you things to make you tear!"

Ron yelled, "We have to get out of here!"

He watched as Roween turned to him and nodded before dropping the doctor to the floor. As the doctor tried to stand, Ron rushed over, punching him in the jaw, knocking him unconscious.

"I don't want any trouble from you, and that wand thing, anymore," Ron said before dragging the doctor up the stairs.

When they reached the top, Roween tugged on his collar and asked where Amanda was.

"They went to Linda's house," Ron replied as he pulled the doctor into the hall.

Roween was off in a flash, disappearing into the night, heading for Linda's home, which was thankfully not far.

As Ron pulled the doctor out of the doorway, the police arrived. He explained who he was and that he was one of the people who called. They had to break in because the doctor was going to torture a little girl. He told them where to find Amanda, and answered questions as authorities put out the fire.

After the flames subsided, one of the policemen approached Ron and the officer questioning him, having confirmed that Amanda was all right. They congratulated Ron on his actions. "The girl confirmed that the doctor had taken her and tied her up. That man over there said that he used something to shock him. He's pretty beaten up; lucky that didn't happen to you. Oh, and he said that some others went to your house for help."

Ron shook his head. "I got thrown around a bit, and he was trying to shock me with something, but I don't think it got me." He didn't know how to say that the doctor used a magic wand that shot lightning.

Thankfully the fire hadn't caused much damage, and the fire department found Linda's dropped phone. "Smart move keeping the phone on. We recorded everything. That guy is going away for a long time."

Ron counted his blessings when someone from the fire department carried out a long stick with spikes. He held it up, telling them, "This is what probably started the fire."

The officer looked at it. "Looks like a homemade cattle prod. Did he get you with this?"

Ron shrugged. "I don't know if that was it, but he did get me a few times."

The officer pressed the button and flinched as a large spark jumped between the spikes.

"You sure you're all right?" he again asked Ron, who nodded he was.

"Just in case, have the paramedics check you out. This thing looks like it could be lethal."

Ron agreed, and they walked with him to the EMTs. "Oh, do you mind if I make a call? We have some friends who were waiting for us," Ron asked. The police thought that was all right and handed him Linda's phone.

* * *

Meanwhile, Edward and Phil arrived at Ron's cabin. Phil

immediately jumped out and pounded on the front door. "Hey, we need your help! The doc's gone crazy! He's got some girl and that fairy thing!"

While Phil yelled, Edward unloaded the device they brought and ran the cable from the truck.

"No one's home, Phil. Best we can do is maybe trade these other creatures for the girl and Grey," Edward said.

Suddenly the door swung open, and they were met by two infuriated brownies.

"Help us. We're trying to save our friend and a girl from the doctor!" Phil exclaimed.

"Are you now?" Erant growled.

Phil nodded and pleaded for them to help. Josclyne felt his pleas to be true.

"Unfortunately, we cannot assist you; we cannot leave this house," she said.

Edward placed the box down on the walkway just as the phone rang. The brownies didn't move, but as the answering machine picked up, they heard Ron's voice. "Hey, guys, sorry we're late; ran into some trouble. But the good thing is, everyone is all right. We'll be there later."

Both brownies turned to face the two men. "Well now; it seems you don't need our help after all." Erant smiled as he looked down at the box on the walkway. "We can only influence things in this house, and those connected to it."

Within seconds, Erant hopped along the cord to their truck. Pushing buttons and using the tools in the back, he started taking it apart. Edward went to move the box but was suddenly lifted into the air by Josclyne. Phil, however, looked at her, seeing the anger in her eyes. "We didn't know this was bad. I'm sorry."

"You have manners, and will be punished by the acceptance of your crimes. This one here, however, worked with that doctor to steal magic; he will be dealt with," Josclyne said as she threw him into the woods, where the sylphs took him away in a whirlwind.

"Are you going to kill him?" Phil asked.

"No, but you won't be able to sit near him for some time," she said.

Phil looked puzzled as she told him to "wait beside the wheeled thing you came here in." But as he approached where they had parked, he saw it in pieces. It had been taken apart bolt by bolt. Erant stood, balanced on the power cord.

"Hey, you, see this thing? If you hunt magic again, this will be you," Erant said.

Phil nodded in fear before sitting down and waiting for the police to arrive.

Edward, however, wasn't so lucky. The sylphs had carried him to the skunk's den and dropped him straight on top. Within seconds, he was met with the back ends of several stomping skunks, who proceeded to spray him all over. The stench was so overpowering that he passed out, and since he was still there, they sprayed him again and again.

Chapter Twenty

It had been three days since the incident at the doctor's house; things had been quiet. Back at Linda's home, there was a knock on the door, which she quickly answered. "Officer Tennent, how are you?"

"We're all done; we've taken care of what remained from the truck at his place," she said, pointing to Ron walking down the hall. "And we've finished our investigation."

Linda smiled, trying not to look suspicious. "What did you find?"

"It was remarkable how fast those two took apart their own vehicle. That doctor must have done something to them to make them go crazy like that," the officer said, as if she were still trying to figure out what had happened to the men.

Linda only nodded; she already knew what had happened. Erant had told them everything about it, having pride in his prowess with mechanical things—or lack thereof. Both Linda and Ron figured the less they said, the better; besides, how do you tell the police that a brownie dismantled a truck and that the other man was whisked away to a skunk's den by sylphs, and doing so without sounding like you were crazy yourself?

Instead, Linda only smiled, then offered the officer some coffee, which was gratefully accepted.

"How are you two doing?" Officer Tennent asked, looking back at the heavy door as it closed solidly behind her. She was referring to the attention both Ron and Linda were now receiving from the town after saving Amanda.

"I think he's almost done writing the article about it," Linda said, causing the woman to laugh.

The officer asked again why they hadn't called the police sooner. Ron only said, "Sometimes you just have to act. We did call after we found Amanda was in danger."

"That doctor is going away for a very long time. But it's the strangest thing. Those other three all have similar stories about magic and creatures."

The officer's statement made Ron choke on his coffee. "You mean, they believe them?"

She looked at him. "Well, they have matching stories, and they all seem to believe they were hunting magical creatures."

Linda started feeling a little uncomfortable and froze when Ron sat up. "Oh, I get it; there were supernatural creatures in my house that took their truck apart. Sounds like they're trying to get the insurance company after me."

The officer had just taken a sip of coffee and almost spat it out trying not to laugh. When she recovered, she said, "I just wanted to let you know that the investigation's done, and the doctor is safely behind bars. So, you can go home if you like."

Ron laughed before looking at Linda. "It's nice here; wouldn't mind a few more days."

The officer smiled. "When you're ready, we have some paperwork for you to sign off on down at the station."

Ron thanked her for stopping by. The woman looked at Linda

with a smile, nodding to her as she walked out the door.

As the heavy door closed, Linda turned to look at Ron; she wasn't smiling.

"You had to say something about house spirits, didn't you?" she scolded.

Ron laughed. "It's not as if they would believe us."

She sat down and cuddled up next to him on the flowered couch. "I'm glad they took their time with the investigation; you got to spend some time here."

Ron looked into her eyes. "I'm glad, too. But I think we should check on things back at my place, don't you? Our other friends may be getting a bit anxious."

Linda agreed.

* * *

Roween was flying room to room, making sure all the plants were doing well. It had been a few days since Ron had been home, and she wanted the place to look as it had when he'd left. The police had looked over the house and surrounding forest. They had found several cameras and some strange devices. When they asked Ron what they were, he always replied, "I don't know; did they put them there?" knowing in reality that they were there to detect magic.

As Roween raced through the house, the brownies came out from hiding.

"I know Ron will be home soon," Josclyne said.

"Hmm . . . can't wait to have that big one walking round here instead of those others," Erant replied.

Roween remained quiet as she neatened up the windowsill, making sure the ginger plant that had been her bed was primped and proper. She only stopped when she saw Ron's truck coming down the road.

Roween sang, "*My friends, they are here, my heart ascends. Let's greet them dear, their absence ends.*"

As they walked in, Ron yelled, "We're home. Anyone here?"

"What are you so happy about, you big one?" Erant grumbled, bringing a tap from his wife.

"How is everyone?" Linda asked.

Roween spun in a pirouette, ending with a bow as Josclyne said, "We are very well."

All laughed after Erant grumbled, "We've had people trampling through here for three days. How do you think we are?"

It was nice having things get back to normal, or such as they could be in a household full of magical creatures. They reminisced, and everyone laughed when Ron again told them how Roween had the doctor hanging in the air after she'd been set free, and how he'd had to drag the man outside to save him. Erant and Josclyne again told them of the truck and what had happened to one of the others at the skunk's den, and all were happy with the outcome. Roween looked at all her new friends as she sat on top of the worn couch between Linda and Ron and smiled before flying to its arm.

She looked around, and the air was full of the warmth of happiness, but her mind was heavy, because a fairy's work is never done. She still smiled, but she had been neglecting the forest. She had friends and others to see, and still many things to do, so she quietly flew to the open window and looked out into the forest. She touched the flower on the windowsill that had been her home for the past few weeks. This home away from home had been filled with fun and flair; she had fulfilled an old promise to Linda and found a new friendship. She again touched the leaf caringly, thanking the ginger plant that had helped her and kept her warm while she healed. But her eyes again wandered out the window into the forest.

"Where are you going?" Roween heard behind her, causing her to spin around abruptly.

"Sorry, didn't mean to startle you," Ron said.

She smiled and said, "*I'm too quick to be caught like a snick,*" before she flew up to his face, tapping his cheek. "*Unfortunately, I must go—many things to do, you know.*"

"I know, you always seem to be leaving. But there is something I meant to ask."

Roween ignored him, quickly flying around to say her goodbyes to everyone before flying out the window. Ron rushed out the door after her; Linda joined him as they stood before their fairy friend. "You didn't let me ask my question."

Linda looked at him. "What question?"

"Why she seemed so much brighter when we saved her from the doctor."

Roween moved closer, and with her magic, pulled the rings she had made for them gently together. But, when her magic stopped, they remained suspended, still being drawn to each other. Roween then gave a glowing fairy smile. Ron couldn't help but notice she again shone brightly before them as she had before.

"*All is good; that I see. Thanks to you, we are free. It will be some time before you again hear my rhyme,*" Roween sang.

She slowly floated toward the forest. "*If only you knew; so many things to do.*"

Both watched and began to wonder when they'd see her again. There was still warmth in their hearts at Roween's words before her glow faded into the flickering shadows of leaves.

"We are friends, and all is right. For we've seen through fire and fight, had adventures, with this humble sprite, through radiant dawns and darkened nights; even finding your heart's delight. For you see a love, ever so bright; that's the true source of a fairy's light."

Ron felt Linda's hand squeeze his and he turned to see a tear in her eye as their fairy friend disappeared into the forest. Although Roween leaving was sad, the smile on Linda's face told him she knew the same as he. Roween wasn't really gone; after all, the forest is a fairy's home, and in time, they knew in their hearts that they were sure to see her again.

Other Books in This Series

Time moves on for all things, especially humans. It also brings new adventure. Amanda and the gang will return in.

The
Raven
Hunters

The world is hiding magic. Amanda, new friends and old, are about to find out that there is much more than they ever thought existed.

ABOUT THE AUTHOR

Stephen has experience in technology, engineering, and sales spanning over 30 years. He has been writing science fiction and fantasy for far longer—his work primarily for role-playing and short stories personally, using his knowledge and imagination within his life. He is always known to have a story to tell and usually with a hint of adventure. Stephen decided to present his first novel for all to see. And through his character's eyes, you may find that life can be an adventure, and it's always better with a bit of magic.